A. ZAVARELLI

Playlist

Reflecting Light—Sam Phillips

In My Veins—Andrew Belle

Taking Pictures—Sam Phillips

Bird Set Free—Sia

Paper Bag—Fiona Apple

I Wish I Could Break Your Heart—Cassadee Pope

Hunter—Dido

Here is Gone—Goo Goo Dolls

Big Girls Cry—Sia

Let Love In—Goo Goo Dolls

Bad Things—Jace Everett

Prologue

Conor

T here are two things my old man always told me were inevitable. Death and captivity. From the moment the hospital stamped my birth certificate, my years have been numbered. It's in my DNA, true as the Irish blood running through my veins.

For as long as I could remember, Pop was in and out of the can. He never could live straight. He tried, a couple of times, but within a week or two of flipping burgers, he'd be back to planning his next big score. I suspect he always knew it would kill him. But when I asked him about it once, he told me he'd rather go down in a blaze of glory than choking on his Jell-O in the nursing home.

When I was a kid, I figured it'd be the same with me. What other choice did I have? I was raised with the notion that the only way to make a living was to jack trucks and rob banks. If you wanted something in this world, you had to take it.

So, standing here as I am, destined to go down in my own blaze of glory, it isn't all that unexpected. Only difference is, it's not a security guard or cop I'm squaring off with, but six members of the Lenox

I

Hill crew.

Best case scenario is that I get one shot off before they do me in, and I have every intention of making that shot count. That greasy fucker with the slicked back hair and beady eyes will have a fat, hot piece of lead lodged in his face if it's the last thing I ever do. Whatever happens after that will be worth it.

I rub the ink on my arm and meet his gaze. The drink in my system almost knocks me on my arse when I reach for my piece. When the adrenaline is high, everything seems faster and more amplified.

My heart is full of thunder and my palms are clammy. I've lived this moment a hundred times over in my mind, unwavering about the way it would go down. But reality is always different than our imaginations. When the piece of shite across the warehouse realizes what's happening, it doesn't bring me relief like I thought it would.

Doubt nags me. A bullet to the head is too quick, a kindness he doesn't deserve. If I'm lucky, I'll only get to enjoy his suffering for a second or two before my own skull is cracked open and splattered in pieces across the cement floor. But when it comes to options I'm all out. His crew is closing in on me as I raise my piece and look him in the eyes.

"For Brady."

There's a flurry of rapid movements as they all reach for their own weapons, and for a moment, I wonder if my Pop would say I'd done good. I could only ever do bad in his books, but I'd like to believe he'd tell me I'd done him proud for this one thing.

And Brady too.

But that fantasy is snatched away from me before I have a chance to make good on it. When gunfire erupts around me, there is only one last horrifying thought. I've fucked this up too because they got to me first.

Any second now, I'll feel the shock of pain and fire when bullets pierce my flesh. One second passes, and then two, and I'm still standing. I haven't fired a single shot, but when I look around me, the Lenox Hill crew are dodging for cover themselves.

I stagger over to the wall and duck behind a partition as I try to piece together what's happening. There's a lot of shouting. A few low moans from somewhere in the corner. I don't know how long it goes on for, but when there's a pause, I stumble out in a panic, seeking out my target. Instead, I'm met with the end of a cold barrel to the back of my head.

"Slow down there, lad," the Irish interloper instructs me. "Where exactly do ye think ye're off to so quickly?"

I try to shake him off as my eyes scour the warehouse for the blue shirt. I find it peeking out from the stack of boxes along the wall and my feet move in that direction before my mind can catch up to logic. I'm about a half a step closer to my goal before the man behind me grabs me again and tosses me to the floor.

"Just let me kill him," I slur. "Then you can put a bullet in me head."

The Irishman narrows his eyes and looks to his companion with the glasses. These guys aren't part of some low life street gang. They're clean cut and hard. The kind of blokes who wear clothes way too nice for this neighborhood. There's no doubt about who and what they are. Given their accents similar to my own, they could only be part of the Irish syndicate.

"Since when did the Lenox Hill crew start running with such jittery lads?" The guy with the glasses asks.

"I'm not with them." I glance over my shoulder, tracking the flash of blue. "And he'll get away if ye don't let me sort him out. You were going to do it anyway, so this is all I ask of ye. Let me be the one to do him in."

The desperation bleeding from my voice mixes with the alcohol in my veins, and it's not a great combination. My words are slurred, my movements slow, and I really don't give a feck who these pricks are. When they don't answer me, I start scuttling backwards on my hands and knees while they watch in amusement.

I

The guy in the leather jacket shakes his head. "Ye have to give him credit for his determination."

His laughter dies when I yank out my piece and swivel around on the floor, too drunk to get up. My arm nearly falters as I take aim at the blue shirt, finger twitching on the trigger. I'm a split second away from firing when the man with the glasses walks up and kicks it from my hands.

"Calm down, lad," he tells me as I scramble for the gun again. "Don't ye know, if ye have beef with this tool... a bullet to the head ain't the way to sort him out."

I pause long enough to look up at him. "Then what would you suggest?"

"That's a fair question," the other man answers. "One that my mate here wouldn't mind explaining to ye. But first thing's first, lad. What exactly did that prick over there do to get ye so jacked up?"

The whiskey in my stomach curdles and I swallow down the bitterness of the raw truth.

"That prick killed my kid brother."

One

Conor

"**W**here in the bleeding hell have you two been?" Crow asks as Rory and I slump onto our bar stools at Sláinte.

The Irish run strip joint is still bumping with energy at this late hour, but I'm limp with exhaustion. Tonight was meant to be a simple drop, but nothing in the syndicate is ever simple. It seems like every other week some new gobshite is gumming up the works.

"Those fucking arseholes hit our shipments again," Rory moans. "The Loco Salva-whatever-the-fuck they call themselves."

"Again?" Crow frowns. "That's the second time this week."

"I doubt they'll be going away anytime soon," I say. "Considering we just took out five of their crew."

Crow's brow furrows like I just reminded him of something, but whatever it is, he doesn't mention it. "Chrissakes, Conor, you still have blood on your face. Go clean yourself up."

Even though I've been with the outfit for a couple years now, I'm still the youngest of the lads. So, when Crow tells me to do something,

I do it. I take my leave and descend into the bowels of the club where the gambling and killing usually take place.

Sometimes it's a pain in the arse being the rookie, but even if it takes a lifetime, I'm willing to prove myself to the brotherhood. Without them, I'd be six feet under, as useless as my father always told me I was. Crow might give me shite most of the time, but he's been offloading a lot more responsibility lately too. At the end of the day, it doesn't matter what he asks of me. I'd lay down my life for this crew, and anything else is just white noise.

That's why I don't hesitate when I finish my business and Crow gestures for me to follow him to one of the private lounges on the balcony. He's quiet as he leans against the railing, eyes scanning the crowd below us.

"Do ye see something that doesn't quite belong here, Conor?"

My eyes move over the sea of faces, and everything is blurry. At this hour, most of the lads are here, drinking and socializing at the end of the busy day. The dancers are the same, just another pair of tits and ass walking about. You'd think a lad would never get sick of looking at it, but you'd be wrong.

I'm tired, and I haven't a clue what this is about, but it must be important. Crow likes to test me from time to time, to see how far I've come since I was just the bumbling kid who stumbled into the middle of one of his gang wars.

There are any number of things he could be talking about. A guy getting too handsy with one of the dancers. Another couple of blokes we've already booted out of here once for being too belligerent. Some sketchy looking customers in the pit, most likely jerking themselves off. But those aren't what catches my eye. And I could be wrong, but it's a gut instinct that I'm not.

The thing that looks most out of place to me is the little birdie hanging out in the back, her fingers beating a nervous rhythm against her table. Under the flashing lights her hair looks almost white, but

I can tell she's a blondie. A wee scrawny thing, by the looks of it. Her chair practically swallows her whole and she can't weigh more than one of my limbs. She looks too fragile to be sitting there by herself and it rubs me the wrong way.

She isn't here to watch the dancers, and she's not trying to pick up clients. So really, she has no business being in the club. Still, I hesitate before I say it out loud, a little unsure of myself. I look to Crow, and he's studying me, waiting for me to get it wrong.

"Well?" he asks. "Spit it out, Conor. I don't have all night."

"The blonde."

Crow tilts his head to the side, a smirk tugging at the corner of his mouth. "What about her?"

"She's not here with anyone. I think she's been in here before, but she doesn't have a reason to be. At least not that I can see."

"Aye, ye're right." Crow says. "She doesn't."

My chest expands, and it feels good that I've done him proud. Crow is my mentor and our superior, and it's important to me that he knows I'm solid. But the levity slips from his face and turns to something darker. I've seen that look before, and I don't like it. Because if Crow isn't happy about it, I won't be either.

"Truth is, I think we have a wee problem, Conor."

"What is it?"

His fingers curl over the railing while he watches her. "She's been hanging around here a lot. Skittish as a fecking mouse. Asked me for a job a couple of times. I suspected something wasn't right about the whole situation from the get go. But then I hear the Locos have been looking for a girl just like her. Apparently, she was the girlfriend of that psycho they called Muerto."

"The one we killed?"

"Aye, that'd be the one," Crow answers. "And I have a reliable source who tells me she was in the house that night."

"Jaysus. You think she saw something?"

3

"I don't know." Crow shrugs. "Dom swears nobody else was in that room when he popped the guy, but I have it on good authority that she was."

His words sink into my gut like a lead weight. If she's a potential witness, it can only mean one thing. The Irish don't leave witnesses behind, and that's what Crow's getting at.

"It's a big ask." He turns to me. "But I'm trusting ye to handle this, Conor. Can I count on you?"

I stuff my hands into my pockets and force my words into submission. "Without a doubt."

He nods solemnly. "I need ye to keep an eye on her. Find out everything ye can about her and what she knows, and don't let her out of your sight. Do what ye need to do to sort this out."

I turn back to the balcony, processing exactly what it is I'm agreeing to. This little birdie is young, probably in her early twenties like me. She's a hot fucking mess who isn't doing herself any favors with the baggy clothes, but even so, it's plain as day she's got a pretty face. It would be a shame to see her killed, but if it comes down to my brothers or her, it's always going to be my brothers.

"How am I supposed to keep an eye on her without raising her suspicions?" I ask.

Crow slaps me on the shoulder and heads for the stairs. "I'm sure you'll sort it out. It shouldn't be too hard, considering I just hired her on as a dancer."

Two

Ivy

I t's been two hours since the guy in the leather jacket told me he'd give me a job. He goes by the name Crow, and I know he runs this club, but I have a suspicion he's in charge of a lot more than that.

He's scary as hell, but the alternative is even worse. That's what keeps me glued to the chair I've been occupying for the last week, hoping and praying nobody will find me here.

The first few times I asked for a job, Crow laughed in my face. But tonight, for reasons I'm not entirely sure of, he finally took pity on me. I could be thinking of the many ways this could go wrong, but right now, I'm just grateful. As risky as this place might be, it's the one place I know the Locos won't come. When you're between a rock and a hard place, it's always wise to choose the lesser of two evils. In my case, that's the Irish fucking mob. They protect their territory with a viciousness that makes any low life gangbanger think twice about crossing this threshold. Now if I can just manage to fly under the radar for a month while I stash away every cent I earn, I can finally leave this city—and all of my bad history—behind.

I'm eager to get started, but apparently Crow isn't on the same page. I've been here all night and the room is starting to spin. I'm tired, cold, and my stomach aches with a pervasive hunger that seeps into my bones. I just really fucking need this job.

A shadow falls over me, and when I look up, I find myself in the crosshairs of a pair of eyes so green they should be illegal. A shiver crawls across my neck as my eyes move over the towering stranger who just entered my orbit unbidden. He's tall, built, and mysterious in a way that only a mafioso could be. I know before he even opens his mouth that this guy is part of Crow's crew. He's as Irish as the day is long, but he's younger than the other guys I've seen lurking around here. Not quite as rough around the edges. His face isn't as weathered, but there's something colder about him. There's a hardness in his features that tells me he's not a man to be easily won over.

He jerks his chin in my direction, eyes narrowed as he examines me. "I'm Conor. Crow sent me to show ye the ropes."

I sit up a little straighter, feeling small and unsure of myself under the weight of his gaze. "Hi. I'm Ivy."

"Ivy." He rolls the name over his tongue with an Irish accent dipped in sin. "That sounds like a made-up name."

"Well, it isn't," I assure him. Even if it is my middle name, it's still my name. I figured it only made sense to use that instead of my first name Elizabeth, which the Locos know me as.

Conor's gaze cuts over my face with laser precision, and whatever he thinks he sees in me makes his lip curl in disgust. Heat climbs up the flesh of my throat and it burns with repressed hate for men like him. Men who think they fucking know me with one glance. I've seen it a thousand times over. They mistake me for weak. A skinny orifice with big boobs and no brains. The misconceptions are endless. I must be a user because I'm gaunt and lifeless, not because I'm starving. I must be a whore because I was with Muerto. Surely, I asked for it.

I've seen it all before. So Conor's quiet judgment means nothing to me, or at least it shouldn't. But for some reason, if I'm being honest, it stings a little more than all the others. Maybe I was wrong, but when our eyes connected, it felt like I saw something else in him. Something other than a mafia asshole.

Regardless, his opinion doesn't matter. I have no interest in a guy like Conor or what he might think of me. The faster I can get the hell away from him and everyone else like him, the better off I'll be.

"What do you need to show me?" I ask, my voice harder than it was just a moment ago.

Conor doesn't budge, and neither do I. He won't take his eyes off me, and I'm too paralyzed to move. He's watching me carefully, waiting for me to crack while he picks me apart until I feel raw inside. My hands squeeze together in my lap in an effort to diffuse the tension, but all I really want to do is curl up in a ball and hide.

Finally, Conor turns and makes a flippant gesture with his hand. "Follow me to the back. I'll show you where the dressing rooms are."

I follow him down the hall, trying to focus on my surroundings, but instead, my gaze bores into Conor. There's a pronounced swagger to his walk that tells me he's confident in his abilities, and granted, he probably should be. He's broad shouldered and built like a fighter, and I could almost bet he looks airbrushed underneath that jacket. His hands are so fucking big he could probably wrap them around my neck twice while he smokes a cigarette and strangles me with two fingers.

I wonder how many people he's killed. And then I wonder something even worse. Is he banging the dancers here every night? Is that why he's in charge? But one look at his stony jaw, and I know that can't be right. He doesn't look like the kind of man who gets enjoyment out of much of anything. He probably fucks like a Viking, tossing women aside when he's done impregnating them with sons for his clan.

I shake myself out of it when he turns to me, and his eyes move over me with a roughness they didn't possess just a few moments before. "I hope ye know how to fix yourself up. That mess ye're sporting now isn't going to fly."

My jaw tightens, but I force a smile, reminding myself how much I need this job. "It's not a problem."

He doesn't seem satisfied with his insult, so he adds salt. "Might want to go heavy on the makeup."

"Duly noted," I bite out. "Lots of makeup."

I don't actually have any makeup, but I'm hoping one of the other dancers will loan me some.

"There's a shower too." He points toward the back of the room. "You should probably use that."

Shame blisters any pride I might have had left, threatening to ruin this opportunity before I even get started. I don't know why he feels the need to be such an ass, but it isn't necessary. I already hate myself enough for both of us, and nothing could be more humiliating than crawling out from behind a dumpster every morning.

I washed up this morning in a gas station bathroom, but it doesn't take a rocket scientist to point out that I still look a fright. My hair is knotted and in desperate need of some hot water and conditioner, and my skin could do with something other than crusty old bar soap.

I cross my arms to hide the fact that I'm shaking. It's freezing in here and with such a low body weight, I get cold easily. "What else do I need to know?"

"You get a three-song set," he says. "Better make it worthwhile. Crow doesn't keep girls around if the clients don't like them."

Christ. I thought I had this job in the bag, but it makes sense that if I screw up, I'm gone. It doesn't matter if I lied and said I have experience; these guys need to believe I do. Thank God I've been camped out here all week watching the other girls because I don't know what I would do out there otherwise.

Conor rakes his eyes over me one last time and shakes his head like he doesn't get why I'm here. "Sort yourself out. You have thirty minutes to impress us, or your arse is out the door."

Three

Conor

"What's up with the new girl?" Rory asks when I sit down beside him in the pit. "Since when does Crow have you managing the dancers?"

"He doesn't." I focus on the stage, so I don't have to look him in the eye. "I offered to do him a favor since he was busy."

Rory studies me as I settle back into the seat and drain my glass. Crow asked me to do this in confidence, so I wouldn't go yapping to all the other lads about it, and I have no intentions of fucking that up.

"She's pretty," Rory observes.

An acerbic taste coats my mouth, tainting my reply with a sharpness I don't recognize. "She looks like Crow pulled her half-dead arse out of a dumpster in Southie."

Rory smirks and relaxes into his seat like he has all bloody night to sit around and watch the dancers. "Suit yourself then. I'm sure there are plenty of others who wouldn't mind having a ride like her."

My jaw hinges shut, and I have the irrational desire to loaf my mate in the head for saying so. As much as I'd like to believe I'm not attracted to the twig of a woman, I can't deny that she would be pretty, once she got cleaned up a little. But just because my dick inflated every time she glared at me doesn't mean shite. She isn't my type. Or anyone in this establishment's type for that matter. Already this assignment is fecking with my head, and the less time she spends here the better.

I'm grateful for the silence when the DJ announces the first dancer of the night. Sláinte is known for having some of the most beautiful dancers in the city, but I can't seem to focus on any of them. One by one, they get up on the stage and perform. They work the crowd and peel away their clothes until there is nothing left but tits and ass. It's an art as old as time, but my dick has fallen asleep, and my irritation is only growing by the second.

Rory is toying on his phone beside me, not paying attention to the show, and I want to know what the feck he's even doing here. He never watches the dancers, and it seems like he's intentionally trying to get on my bleeding nerves. I want to be alone when Ivy comes out. If Rory catches me staring, he'll get the idea that this is something other than what it really is.

By the time the DJ finally announces her, I'm wound up tighter than a coil. Rory, on the other hand, seems content to stuff his phone in his pocket and watch the show when the lights dim and #1 Crush by Garbage blasts from the speakers.

My fists contract as the waifish silhouette moves toward center stage. Her hips sway in a slow, sensual rhythm with every step she takes, arousing the reverence of the crowd. On top of her platform heels, she's a delicate little doll. Her grace is softer than I expected, and a hushed quiet falls over the room as every pair of eyes become enchanted. I'd be lying if I said I wasn't too, and that's a fucking problem.

My cock comes back to life with a craving so violent, I haven't a clue what to make of it. I feel Rory's eyes on me, but I can't look away from her. She's rendered me useless under her spell, along with fifty other men in the room.

I release a breath when the intro finally ends, and the spotlight comes on. The crowd rumbles with excitement, and for a split second, Ivy halts, blinded and stunned. She's cleaned up, just as I instructed, her blonde hair falling in silky waves to the delicate curve of her arse. She's wearing a strappy black outfit she pulled out of the free for all bin, and her eyes are covered in glitter. She's done exactly what I asked and pulled herself together, so I can't figure out why I'm so bloody out of sorts over it.

Fecking Christ.

She's a treat on a cold Boston evening and the crowd loves her. They shout out encouragement, and she starts dancing again. Her body is stiffer, the goddess behind the shadows a faint memory, at least until she closes her eyes and gets lost in the feeling.

There's a part of me I can't rationalize with that doesn't want her to be good at this. I want Crow to say that she's finished. She can do anything else except dance. It isn't logical, and I can't understand it. Especially when she's everything I hate in a woman.

She's so gangly, it leaves little doubt in my mind she's a user. I've been down that road before, and it leaves a sour taste in my mouth even thinking about it. I can't just sit here and watch her undress. I can't watch her sell herself out for cash only to inject it in her arm.

I stand up and swipe my empty glass from the table, itching for another drink. If there's one thing that's certain, I don't need to see what she looks like naked to get the job done. Crow asked me to keep an eye on her, and I will.

And when he asks me to dim the light from her eyes, I'll hand her the fucking needle myself.

Four

Ivy

By some miracle, I managed to survive. I'm still on that adrenaline high when I walk out of the dressing room with all my cash in hand. Even after the house fee, there's a lot of money here. Enough that it gives me hope I can actually make my dream come true. A few more weeks of this, and I'll be solid.

I nearly smash into a broad chested man in the hall, and he winks at me with a playful smile as he helps me gather the jacket I just dropped. "Alright there?" he asks in a cheeky Irish accent.

"Yes, sorry. I didn't see you there."

He flashes a dimple when his lips tilt up. "I liked your routine. Ye did a grand job up there."

"Thanks." I smile. "I was a bit nervous, but I think it went okay."

He offers me his hand. "I'm Rory by the way."

I shake his hand and offer my name reluctantly. I'm not here to make friends, but it's pretty obvious this guy is a part of Crow's outfit.

"Conor and I were just about to grab a bite to eat," he says.

I

"Would ye care to join us?"

I hesitate, uncertain how to navigate this terrain. I need this job, which means playing nice with these guys even though it's the last thing I want to do.

"No funny business." Rory holds up his hands. "Just dinner. Our treat."

I offer him a weak nod. It's not like I can refuse a free meal. Not when I've been existing on one a day if I'm lucky. "Okay, I guess dinner would be alright, as long as it's just dinner."

He holds up two fingers. "Scout's honor."

I follow him to the front of the club where Conor is sitting at the bar. His head is bowed forward, attention on the counter when he senses us approaching him. When he turns to find Rory beside me, his eyes darken and the muscle in his neck twitches. "What's the deal with Twiggy?"

"Ivy," I correct him with a glare.

Rory smirks. "Ivy here is coming to dinner with us. Isn't that nice?"

Conor doesn't seem at all pleased with the idea. His eyes are fixated on me, and he looks like he wishes I would just disappear. I don't know what his problem is, but he's got it out for me. I know I should look away and just let it go, but I can't. There is something about those damning green eyes that render me immobile. I've never felt this kind of tension with anyone else. It's so raw and intense it makes me feel weird all over.

The edgy silence persists until Rory clears his throat and I'm on the verge of telling them both I've changed my mind when Conor grunts. "Let's get after it then."

They take me to a place just down the street, an all-night diner that serves round the clock breakfast, and it's exactly what I need. It has two of my favorite things—food and warmth. But just a few minutes after we arrive, I learn there's something else on the menu.

The waitress seems to know the guys by name, and she offers them a flirtatious smile before her eyes drift over Conor in a not so subtle fashion. Her attention doesn't leave him the entire time we order, and I find myself wondering if there's some history there, and then I wonder why I even care. To my amusement, Conor doesn't return her warmth. In fact, he never takes his eyes off me, and when the waitress finally does look my way, she can't hide her displeasure.

When she disappears to put in our order, Rory chuckles under his breath. "Ye have to give the woman credit. She's persistent."

Conor doesn't laugh or even bother with a reply. There seems to be some tension blooming between the two men, and the conversation remains sparse while we wait for our food. Meanwhile, Conor makes it his objective to toss accusatory glances between Rory and me, but it makes little difference. All I'm concerned with is shoveling the mile-high stack of pancakes I ordered into my mouth when it finally arrives.

When I set down my fork a few minutes later and wipe my mouth with a napkin, Rory laughs and Conor glares. A flush creeps over my face when it occurs to me how crude that must have been. I didn't even stop to think. I just ate until there was nothing left on my plate.

"Must have been hungry," Rory muses.

"I was," I admit sheepishly.

"Drugs will do that to you," Conor growls as he slides out of the booth and yanks out his wallet. "I guess it's my treat tonight."

I curl into myself as he retreats, and Rory finishes up his plate. "Don't worry about him. Kid can be a grouchy motherfucker sometimes."

I glance down at my worn-out Chucks and nod. "I don't do drugs, just so you know."

Rory bobs his head like it wasn't even a question, and then we sit in awkward silence while I try to figure out what to do next. It's freezing outside, and I'm tempted to use some of my shiny new cash to pay for a hotel room for the night. But I don't want to dip into any of it. Not when I think of what's at stake.

"Conor and I were thinking about playing some cards tonight." Rory peers at me over the rim of his coffee cup. "Fancy joining us?"

My fingers tangle together in my lap as I consider his offer. I don't know these guys from Adam. The smart choice would be to decline. But logic isn't as desperate as basic human needs, and the thought of hunkering down behind a garbage can in the freezing cold for the rest of the night has me thinking it might be alright. Even just a few hours off the street would do me some good. Between the cold temperatures and the Locos scouring the city for me, I'm not really in a position to turn it down.

My eyes drift over to Conor, who is still talking to the waitress up at the register. He catches me staring, and I swallow down the weirdness I feel. He offers her a smile like he's trying to goad me and I turn my attention back to Rory. I only just met them, but I guess I should feel secure in the fact that neither of them seems to want anything from me.

"Sure. I guess I could play some cards."

Five

Conor

Fecking Rory.

He pulls this shite just to get his jollies off. The guy can get any chick he wants, but there's only ever been one he's head over heels for. Since she's not around right now, I guess he's got nothing better to do with his time than fuck with me.

He makes small talk the entire drive back to his place, laying it on real thick with Ivy. He asks her what sort of music she fancies and tells her jokes and does all the things that makes him irresistible to women, and I can't be arsed to participate when he tries to involve me in the conversation.

I don't want them getting buddy buddy, but I can't come right out and open my gob about what's going on either. Crow asked me to do this quietly for a reason, and I won't betray that. But I can't say it doesn't bother the hell out of me to watch Rory turning on his charm and making Ivy laugh. Once we're inside the house, I last about ten minutes before I can't stomach another second of it.

"I've got a phone call to make," I announce.

Rory arches his eyebrow at me in challenge. He wants me to come right out and say it, like I've caught feelings for this bird or something. He best not be holding his breath.

I walk outside and stare at my phone, but the whole excuse was bollocks. There is no call. I just don't have it in me to be hanging around with a girl who'll probably be dead before the week's end. And I'm not in the sort of mood to stay and watch Rory win her over either. I don't even really know what I'm doing when I get into my car and drive away, but for now the further I can get from her the better.

I drive around the city and fuck off until the early hours of morning, doing nothing in particular. By the time I get back to Rory's, all the lights are off, and Ivy's passed out on the sofa.

For a minute, I just stand there and look at her. It would make my life a lot easier if I could find a reason to hate her, but right now, I can't. She's so young. Too young to be heading for the grave. And she's too fucking pretty to be hanging out with the lot of us. Shaking her ass up on stage and disrespecting herself to feed her addiction.

A girl like her should be somebody's wife. She should be safe at home in the suburbs, making a life for herself. Or going to school. Or, fuck, I don't know. But she shouldn't be here right now. She shouldn't be mixed up with the likes of us, or the Locos, or anyone else this side of Boston.

Regardless of what I said about her earlier, I can't deny how goddamned beautiful she is. I see it every time I look at her face, and then I hate her for it. She knows it too. She knows I want her to disappear. But I can't seem to stop fucking staring at her. Craving something I shouldn't be craving. I'm not like Rory. I don't thrive on the attention women give me. I've done just fine without a woman in my life or my bed for the last few years, and I've no intentions of changing that now.

But I could make her laugh. I could make her smile at me, if I really wanted to. It's just that I don't. I can't think of her that way. I can't humanize her when fate has other plans. It's better if she hates me. It's better if she thinks I'm an arsehole because in the end, I'll have no choice.

The back of my eyelids feel like glue, and when I peel them open, it comes as no shock that I find myself in a dark, cold basement. I might have been shitefaced last night, but I remember it clearly. I accepted my fate when I set out to kill the man who killed my kid brother, and the light of day won't change that.

A newly familiar face comes into focus as he kneels down in front of me and pokes me in the cheek. It's the man with the glasses and the suit.

"Morning," he says. "I've been waiting all night for ye lad."

"Ye missed out on half the fun already," the other man says.

I haven't a clue what they're talking about, so I just nod, which I figure is what most guys probably do when they speak.

"I'm Crow," the man in the leather jacket introduces himself. "And this is my mate, Fitzy. But you can call him Reaper."

"I'm Conor," I mumble around the dryness in my mouth.

Crow tosses me a bottle of water, and I crack it open and sit up slowly, the room still spinning from my hangover.

"So, what now?" I ask.

The men look to each other and then back to me.

"Ye had a fair bit to drink last night." Crow cocks his head to the side and examines me. "So why don't ye tell me again what that fella in the blue shirt did to get ye so worked up."

I grind my jaw together and stare down at my shoes, noticing the tiny splatters of crimson that weren't there before. The urge to retch is strong. It isn't the sight of blood, but the smell that makes me sick. And even if it is dry, I swear that phantom scent is there in my nose. I kick off my shoes and push them beneath the chair where I don't have to see them.

"He killed my brother."

"Ah, so he did." The way Crow says it still sounds like a question, but when Fitzy bobs his head, that question is settled.

Crow scrubs a hand through his hair and shrugs. "Well, lad… the way I see it is you have two choices. I'm sure if ye think on it, ye're quite aware of the predicament we're in now, having ye alive and all."

"I'm not a snitch," I tell them. "I wasn't concerned with what your crew was doing last night."

"So ye say," Fitzy scoffs. "But so does every bloke who passes through this basement."

I glance around the room and take it all in. It's nothing fancy, just four walls and a bunch of tables littered with cards and remnants of cigars. In other words, the home base for their underground gambling establishment. Just like the ones my Pop used to tell me about. He lost a finger in one of these once.

"Maybe you could keep me around." I gesture to the tables. "I'm a gambling man meself, and I know how to deal."

Crow laughs and doesn't try to hide it. "Tell ye what, kid. We're going to do ye a solid. Ye asked to kill the clown in the blue shirt, aye?"

I nod.

"Well, my pal Reaper here, he's going to show ye the ropes. Help ye kill him real good. I suspect you'll be pleased with the results."

It almost sounds too good to be true, but I play along. "Okay."

Crow goes on. "The lad will die, and you can do whatever ye want to him. Anything your dark little heart desires. Only thing is, when we're through, Fitzy's gonna have to do ye in as well. But he'll make it easy on you."

Silence falls over the room as they both study me, waiting for a response. They're probably waiting for the fall out. Some moaning and pleading and even a few tears maybe, but I've got none of that to barter with.

"You've got yourself a deal."

Crow's lips flatten, and Fitzy gives me a respectable nod like I'm a man of honor. I've never considered that I was until now, and it feels pretty fucking righteous. My Pop was always bitching about me being too weak, and I just wish he were here to see it. If I'm going to die, I think it's a fair shake. I'll get what I want, and what I expected anyway.

"Alright lad." Fitzy bends down and helps me up off the floor. "I suppose we should go ahead and do this then, aye?"

"Aye, I'm ready."

Crow slaps me on the back and squeezes my shoulder. "Have fun then, lad. And try not to chuck."

I've never killed a man. And before Brady, I never really gave it too much thought either. Pop told me he'd killed a couple of guards in his day. They'd get in the way, sometimes, he said. Trying to be a hero cost them their lives. Hearing these sorts of stories made me think it ran in my blood. Something had me convinced that I was just as hard as Pop was, and when it came time, I could do it too. But that was all before I met the Reaper. He's the one with the glasses and an emotionless face.

The man is clean cut and as precise as a surgeon the way he moves about the little room where our prisoner waits. He discards his suit jacket and rolls up his shirt sleeves while he listens to classical music. It seems like an awfully weird fucking way to prepare to murder someone, but it looks like he's probably done it at least a hundred times over.

The guy I've been waiting six months to kill is already strapped to a table, mouth gagged, shirt cut off. There isn't an ounce of fear in his eyes when he looks at me. The Reaper, though, that's a different story. Albie knows, just as I do, something isn't quite right with this Fitzy character. He's too stiff. Too formal. And way too calm. I feel sick all over again when he turns and gestures for me to come look at his selection of tools.

"Pick your pleasure."

I take a gander at the metal contraptions, but I only recognize a few. Reaper must sense it, because he hands me a pair of shears. "I suggest starting with the fingers and toes. Makes it real for them."

Jaysus.

I turn back to Albie, and he's laughing at me with his eyes. Even he knows I don't have the stomach for something like this.

"Do ye think he made your brother suffer?" Reaper asks.

I have half a notion to tell him to fuck off, but he has a point. The entire reason I set out to do this in the first place is because Albie made Brady suffer. And for what? Because he fucking could.

"He tortured him," I answer, my voice barely audible.

"Then it's time to return the favor, lad. One last act before ye go. Would it not give ye peace to know you'd done what ye set out to?"

Reaper's words give me the conviction I need, and I move to the table. He follows with a metal bowl in his hands, setting it beside Albie. "For the appendages."

He applies a tourniquet, which never would have occurred to me, and then steps back to let me get after it. Albie's taunting me with his eyes, still not convinced I can do it. I think of Brady, recalling how his face was so mangled I couldn't even hold a viewing for him before the service.

From the time he was just a wee lad, it fell upon me to look after him. I fed him, clothed him, made his lunches for school. He was a good kid with a heart of gold. He would have done anything to fit in. All he ever wanted was to feel like he had a family other than the shitty hand we were dealt. I hoped if I guided him in the right direction and stuck by his side it would be enough. But in the end, I failed him.

"He was just a kid." I meet Albie's dead eyes. "A fucking kid."

His lips twist beneath the duct tape, and I can tell he's smiling when I reach for his hand. It's all a bleeding joke to him. But it stops being funny when the shears close around his index finger and I start to squeeze.

It's a lot harder than I expected. There's a crunch of bone and tissue before a tortured groan rumbles from Albie's chest. Blood starts to seep from the wound, dripping onto the floor and making a real mess of what I'm trying to do. I can't seem to get through the bone.

"It takes a wee bit to get the technique down," Reaper tells me. "Just give it a good hard squeeze."

I do. I close my eyes and squeeze it like I wanted to squeeze that trigger the night before, and the nub of his finger falls to the floor with a satisfactory thud.

"Good on ya, lad." Reaper pats me on the back. "Only nineteen more to go."

He leaves me to it, and I'm surprised to find it gets a little easier each time. Albie's squirming against the table, moaning and whining and carrying on like the pussy he is. Blood sprays my face and clothes, but I can't smell it anymore. It's like I'm in a trance and all I can hear is the sound of Albie's pain. I like it a lot more than I expected to.

The door opens, and another guy walks in. He's got a bowl full of stew of some sort, which he continues to eat while he watches.

"Rory." Reaper greets him.

"Fitz."

Rory finishes his food and then sets the bowl aside, leaning back against the counter in the same fashion as the Reaper. "What's the deal with this bloke?"

"They were both at the warehouse last night," Reaper explains. "One on the table killed his kid brother."

"Look at him go." Rory eyes me off. "Kid's a natural. What's your name lad?"

"Conor." I nod to him and then continue on with my work. I've still got four toes to get through and Albie's screaming like a banshee now, *nearly choking on his own tongue.*

"Conor," Rory muses. "Ye might just have yourself a new apprentice, Fitz."

Reaper's response is dry and to the point. "He'll chuck when he's through."

"We all chucked the first time," Rory says.

Reaper shrugs. "Crow gave him a deal anyhow. The lad won't be sticking around."

The room goes silent. When I glance at Rory, the amusement has disappeared from his face. He doesn't like the sound of this deal, but I don't know why he cares one way or another.

"The lad was in agreement," Reaper clarifies.

"He's a fucking kid," Rory mutters under his breath. "Does Niall know about this?"

Silence. Again.

They don't say anything else when I turn away, but the door shuts, and I know they're both outside discussing the situation. I don't let it ruffle my feathers. I gave them my word, and if there's one thing my Pop beat into me over the years, it's that a man has to stay true to his word.

My word is all I've ever had, and besides, it's not like there's anything left for me here. Ma's dead. Pop and Brady too. I've been wandering this city without an ounce of purpose for months and I'm tired. Sammy was the only thing I had left, and she sure as fuck didn't give a shite about me when I caught her banging some random bloke in the alley last month for a fix. Doesn't matter anyway. She's gone now too. Took her last needle to the arm a couple weeks ago.

I put those thoughts out of my mind as the last of Albie's toes fall into the bowl. When Reaper comes back, Rory is gone, and that suits me just fine.

"Alright, lad," he says. "How do ye feel about blow torches?"

Six

Conor

I wake with a start, shaking myself out of the past as my eyes scan the surroundings of my present. The dream doesn't come as a surprise, I have them often. I'll never forget how that night changed my life, but sometimes, it does well to have a reminder. It's trying to come back down to earth that's the hard part. But when I glance around Rory's apartment, I know I've come a long way since I first killed a man in that dingy basement at Sláinte.

Ivy is still on the couch, snoring, and Rory is on the floor. My eyes move between the two of them, and I'm irrationally bent out of shape when I think about what might have happened in my absence last night. Then I realize how ridiculous that notion is, and I try to focus on the task at hand.

I'm not here to worry about whose bed Ivy wants to warm at night. I'm here to see what she knows, and I start by digging through the bag she carries with her. All that turns up are an extra set of clothes, a few toiletries, and her cash from last night.

No needles. No drugs.

My eyes move over her face, and I know I can't be wrong about this. She's too thin. If it isn't needles, it must be pills. I take a peek at her arms, and there aren't any marks that I can see, but that doesn't mean shite. There are a million other places to inject.

I blow out a breath and toss her shit back into her bag before nudging Rory with my boot. He mumbles incoherently, and I nudge the fecker again. When that doesn't work, I blast him with some ice-cold water from the kitchen. He told me to wake his arse up, and I've never been happier to oblige. It's the least he deserves after bringing Ivy back here last night. Rory comes up swinging, and I shield myself behind the couch.

"Real gentleman ye are." He scowls. "Hiding behind a lady."

My lip curls and I can't hide it. "Yeah, a real lady."

Rory grins at my bitter tone, and then a laugh bursts from his chest. "I brought her home for you, ye fucking muppet. I saw the way ye were making eyes at her all night long. But then ye disappeared and couldn't be bothered to come back here to sort her out."

My chest expands, and I shouldn't be so relieved by his dumbarse admission. I have no right to that feeling, not with her. I'd do well to remember that.

"Get her some breakfast and then give her a lift home," Rory says.

I want to tell him to feck off, but I keep my gob shut as he disappears down the hall and I nudge Ivy. She doesn't budge, so I poke at her arm again, and still nothing. Acid coats my lips as I wait for her chest to swell. She was just snoring a few minutes ago.

My fingers come to rest on the soft flesh of her throat, waiting for a pulse. And when I feel the quiet tremor of warm blood pumping through her veins, it hits me like a ton of fucking bricks. I shouldn't care. It shouldn't make a lick of difference when her eyes fly open and lock onto mine, but it does.

"What is it?" She eyeballs the hand that's still on her throat, then darts upright to check that her clothes are still there. "What's going on?"

"It's morning." I retreat from her and try to find my bearings. "Time to go. I'll sort ye out some coffee and then drop you wherever ye need to be."

"Right." She clears her throat and stares at the floor. "I should probably do that."

I warm up the car while she puts herself together in the bathroom, and she joins me a few minutes later. She looks different this morning with the makeup scrubbed free from her face and her hair pulled back. The sexualized dancer from last night is gone, and all that's left now is sweet. She looks like the kind of girl a guy would want to take home to his mammy.

I force the car into gear and pull onto the street. "Hope you like Dunkies. It's about the only place we ever do breakfast."

I feel her eyes on me before she answers. "Dunkies is fine."

The silence between us doesn't improve, so I opt for the drive-thru to make it as quick and painless as possible. "What do ye fancy?"

She looks at the menu and shrugs. "Just a donut and coffee would be fine."

She's trying to make it easy, and I wonder if it's because she knows I think she's a nuisance. As if I haven't already made that clear. But I remember how she scoffed down her pancakes last night, so with that in mind, I order a mixed dozen and two coffees. I hand them off to her and pull back onto the road.

"Where are we going?" I ask.

"Oh, um, you can just drop me at Sláinte. I left my car there."

"Right, I'll do that then."

We're both quiet, and I can't get there soon enough. I have half a notion to let Crow know this task doesn't suit me, but that would make me a fucking muppet to say so. I barely know this girl. Crow has asked so little of me, and this is the only thing he's ever asked me to do in confidence. I'm not about to let down the man who took me in and gave me a purpose over a bloody woman.

"Where did you go last night?" Ivy pipes up.

I look at her, and her cheeks flush with pink when she realizes how stupid her question is. You don't ask a mafia bloke where he goes. Ever. She would know that from her time with Muerto, I'm sure, but she doesn't retract the question.

"Out." I grip the steering wheel tighter. "I had business."

"We waited for you to come back," she tells me. "I thought we were going to play cards. Wasn't that the whole point?"

"I didn't invite you," I point out.

She turns toward the window, and I feel like an arsehole. But it's better this way. She should know what she's getting herself into.

A few minutes later she appears to have bounced back from it when she opens the box of donuts. "Which one do you want?"

"None. Those are for you."

I feel her eyes on me, studying me like she could figure me out, but she doesn't say anything else. The drive back to the club is the longest one I've ever made, and when I pull into the empty lot, I can finally breathe again.

"I'm just down the street," Ivy says. "You don't have to wait."

"I'm not," I grumble. "I've got business inside."

"Oh, right. Well thank you for breakfast, and the lift. I guess I'll see you around."

We both get out of the car, and I'm tempted to watch her walk away, but instead I turn toward the club and head for the back entrance. Only, I don't go inside. I wait until Ivy is out of sight and then start to follow her, crossing the street and using the cover of the parked cars on the other side and a wide distance to stay hidden.

She checks over her shoulder often as she walks, but never catches sight of me. I wonder if she senses that I'm the monster on her heels, or if it's someone else she's looking for. Her steps quicken, and she legs it several blocks like a thief in the night, darting over broken footpaths and between shoddy buildings. We're in a commercial district now, and Ivy takes a visible breath when she crosses over the threshold as if it were her saving grace.

The wheels are turning in my mind, trying to sort out her motivations for being here. But a minute later, that mystery is solved on its own. Ivy checks both ways to make sure nobody is watching as she disappears down another alley. It's not a throughway. It's three brick walls merged together and a bunch of garbage cans. The kind of place that the homeless usually sleep. Or the kind of place that addicts like to shoot up. Except, she didn't have anything on her this morning, which only leaves me with more questions.

For the next hour, I watch and wait, but she never comes out. My mind goes to a dark place, wondering if she's passed out cold. Wondering if she'll even be alive when I check on her. Jaysus. It's too much, and I don't have the patience to sit here all bloody day.

I leg it down the alley and peek around the corner of the garbage can, and there she is. Laying on a fecking piece of cardboard with a shabby ass blanket to keep herself warm. Her eyes are closed, and she's asleep like this is the most normal thing in the world for her. It's an image I won't soon forget.

Whatever she may have seen or done in her past, she shouldn't be living this way. Not like an animal. Not like this is all she deserves.

This isn't fecking right, and I want to do something about it. But then I think of Crow and my brothers in the syndicate. Everything they've done for me. I promised him I would take care of this, and helping the girl isn't going to help anyone. Not if she has a ticking clock on her life anyway.

Christ.

I wipe a hand over my face, and she twitches, her brows pinching together like she's having a bad dream. From the looks of it, her whole life is a bad dream. I need to get out of here. I need to put some distance between us before I do something stupid.

I walk back out of the alley and resume my watch from across the street, trying to erase the image of her sleeping on the ground like a dog.

I can't help her. She's the one who decided to get wrapped up with the Locos. She's the one who walked straight into the lion's den, knowing what fate waited for her if Crow found out. She's the one who's been fucking with my head since she came into my life.

This is on her.

Seven

Ivy

The blistering cold has seeped into my bones by the time I wake, and even though I'm tempted to go back to sleep, I need to move around.

The exhaustion never leaves me. I don't know if it's the hell of the last year or the constant hunger pains, but it's obvious I won't be able to continue on like this much longer. When I think about my reality—the fact that I'm sleeping in an alleyway behind a dumpster with one sack of clothing to call my own—I want to break down and cry. In fact, I do. It's become my morning ritual. But when I'm done, I always manage to pick myself up and carry on, knowing that it won't be like this forever. Soon, everything will be okay.

A glance at my watch confirms that it's still early, and I have almost the entire day to waste before I go back to work tonight. Realistically, I should be looking for another part time job in the day time, but so far, that hasn't panned out. I guess people aren't too eager to hire you when you show up in a pair of tattered jeans and a hoodie.

I stand up and shake out my limbs as I try to figure out what to do. There are a lot of things I could be doing, but most of them are too risky. Unlike the other homeless in this city, the shelters and foodbanks aren't an option. Not when the Locos are looking for me. I don't want anyone else getting hurt because of me, and that's exactly what would happen if I chose to go that route. They want me dead, and they aren't the kind of men who will spare anyone in the process, innocent or not.

There was a brief moment after Muerto's death when I considered going to the cops. I had nowhere else to turn, and everything had been stolen from me. My entire life was gone, and I found myself suddenly free with only a handful of options, each one of them a potential disaster. But I couldn't forget what happened the last time I went to the cops. In the end, I was still on my own. A piece of paper wasn't going to protect me from the Locos or anyone else. It was up to me, and me alone.

Every day that I'm out on the street is a gamble, but it's one I'm willing to take for a better life. And even though I know I shouldn't, I want to take another gamble today. Jumping on a bus and heading up interstate 93 to New Hampshire is the only thing that makes me feel alive anymore. It's been three days already. Too long, and yet not long enough. Every visit is a risk, but I can't live without them.

I stash my belongings behind the dumpster and gather up my cash from the night before, zipping up my flimsy jacket and throwing on my hood and the sunglasses I plucked from a table at Sláinte. The bus station is a short walk, but every step feels like a mile.

Out of habit, I check over my shoulder often, never able to shake that feeling I'm being watched or followed. But this early, in this part of the city, everything is still quiet.

I make it to the station intact, and an hour later I'm nestled into the back of the bus where I can keep an eye on everyone. It's a sparse crowd this time of day, and I'm tempted to nod off again, but I don't.

I can't let my guard down. Not when it comes to these trips. If anyone even looks twice at me, I won't hesitate to jump off and head back to Boston.

The bus arrives just a little past eleven, and my joints creak with the stiffness that comes from sleeping on a cold ground when I get off. But one sniff of the New Hampshire air makes all my aches and pains disappear. I can't contain the smile that tugs at my lips as I beat it down the sidewalk and begin my four-block journey on foot.

I'm grateful that Conor took pity on me and bought an entire box of donuts this morning because without them I'd be feeling pretty weak right about now. Trying to dissect that kind gesture can only lead to a headache, especially when he's insistent on reminding me that he hates me.

The man is confusing, to say the least. One minute he acts like I'm nothing, and the next I catch him staring at me with an intensity that could melt the sun. I've already caught myself giving him way more thought than I can afford, but I can't and won't let myself get caught up with a guy like him. Not when I have so much at stake. I'm reminded of that when I find myself on the doorstep of the beautiful white house with the red door.

I ring the bell, and Lacey checks the video intercom before she opens it. "How are you sweetie?"

"I'm good," I offer an automatic lie.

Lacey doesn't question it. She knows I'm not good, but she also knows better than to delve into it. She's an old friend from my beauty school days, but our lives have gone in wildly different directions. She married a rich stock broker and stays at home now, and I landed myself in the sites of Muerto. Enough said.

She gestures me inside. "He's upstairs. He'll be so excited to see you."

I follow her in and she takes my coat with a frown. "You need something thicker than this. It's freezing out there."

"I know," I mumble. "I just grabbed this in a hurry."

Another lie. It's all I have, but Lacey has already done so much for me. The last thing I need is her feeling like she needs to supply me with clothing too.

"Archer, will you come down here please?" She calls up the stairs.

I wait anxiously as the small footsteps bound across the upper level and down the stairs, and when his face comes into view, I almost burst into tears again.

"Hey baby." I kneel down and brace for impact as the little angel with brown hair and blue eyes flings himself into my arms.

"Hey mama!" he squeals as he buries his face into my neck. "I missed you."

I choke down a sob as I squeeze him in my arms. "I missed you too. So much."

"Are you hungry?" Lacey asks. "I could fix us all some lunch."

"No." I pull Archer up and hold him against my hip. Even though he's getting too big for this at four years old, I can't help it. "I think if you don't mind, we might go down to the park and play for a while."

"Of course." Lacey nods in understanding. These moments with Archer are so precious that I don't want to waste one second of them. "Let me grab his coat and gloves."

Five minutes later, Archer and I are walking hand in hand down to the local park. It's a nice community, and I'm grateful that he's here. This is a safe place for Archer. Far away from Boston and in a house that's secured like Fort Knox. Something Lacey insisted on when she had her own son.

"Tell me what you've been doing." I help Archer onto the swing set and give him a little push.

He flutters his legs and shrugs. "We built an airplane."

"You did?"

He smiles. "Lego airplane."

My heart warms at his happy, easygoing expression, and I can only hope that in the end, when we come out of this, he will be okay. I hope someday he will understand that everything I've done is to keep him safe.

"Mommy got a new job," I tell him. "Do you know what that means?"

"What?" He curls his arms around the chains and stares up at me with a face untainted by the darkness in this world.

"We're going to be together very soon."

He beams at me with a smile that could melt even the iciest of hearts. "Really? Can I bring my Legos?"

I laugh as tears spring to my eyes. "Yes, you can bring all your toys."

For the next hour, we burn out all his energy and mine while I chase him around the park and utilize every square inch of the playground. It amazes me every time I come here to see how much he's grown and changed. Even if it's only been a few days, it seems like a lifetime.

As happy as I am to see him, it's always bittersweet because I know it will be over soon and I'll have to leave him again. And as much fun as we're having, I can't help the nagging sensation of doom in my gut. It's potent today, and I find myself glancing around the park more often than usual, seeking out potential threats. Archer even asks me several times what I'm looking at, and I try my best to assure him that everything is okay, but I can't shake that awful feeling that we're being watched. As we're leaving, it finally becomes apparent why.

Acid burns the back of my throat when I recognize the black BMW with Massachusetts plates parked across the street. I don't know how long he's been there, but when our eyes lock through the window, I know he's done hiding.

"Please." I shake my head as terror clogs my voice. "Please, no."

Conor rolls down the window and gestures to the passenger seat. "Get in."

I shake my head again, and Archer looks up at me. "What's wrong, mama?"

"Nothing, sweetheart." I give him a smile for his benefit. "Everything is just fine."

"Don't make a scene." Conor's lips flatten. "Just get in the car. It's too bloody cold for you two to be out here like this."

I'm trying not to lose my shit, I really am. But my son. He's seen my son. My whole world is crumbling, and I don't know how to handle this. No matter what, I lose.

Conor opens the door and gets out of the car, letting me know he's done fucking around. I don't want Archer to be afraid, and running is pointless. I cling to Archer's hand with mine, desperately trying to think of a solution. My legs feel weak, and my heartbeat is thrashing in my ears. I don't know Conor well enough to understand his character. But what else do I really need to know about him?

He's mafia.

The mafia that I convinced myself it would be a great idea to go work for. "Please," I whisper. "Leave him out of this."

"Ivy," Conor's voice softens as his eyes meet mine. "Your son is safe. On that, I give ye my word."

I pull Archer into my side, wanting so badly to believe it's true. But Conor can see my doubt isn't going anywhere, and he takes matters into his own hands, kneeling down so he's face to face with my baby.

"Hello there, wee fella." He ruffles Archer's hair with his big hand. "My name is Conor, what's yours?"

Archer giggles. "You have a funny accent."

Conor's lip tilts at the corner. "I know, aye."

Archer puffs up his chest proudly. "I'm Archer. And I'm four years old."

"Glad to meet ye, Archer," Conor says. "Ye must be cold. What do ye say we sort ye out a hot chocolate to warm up those bones?"

Archer nods eagerly, and my body turns to stone when Conor takes him by the hand and leads him toward the car.

"Conor, I—"

"Get in." Conor shoots me a look that warns me not to fight him on this. "I promised the boy some hot chocolate. If ye're good, I'll buy you one too."

I watch helplessly as he buckles Archer in, debating my options. But the truth is, I'm out of them. Conor knows about him, he's seen him, and there's only one way out of this. I'm going to have to make a deal with the devil. I'll need to talk my way out of this. Make him promises, blood sacrifices, give him my body. Whatever it takes. Because I can't go through this again. I can't lose Archer again.

Conor presses his hand against my lower back and urges me forward, leading me around to the passenger side. He helps me in, and then buckles me in, hesitating only briefly as he looks up at my face. There is a softness in his eyes I've never seen before, and it scares me. It scares me because it makes me feel like I can trust him, and that's the worst possible mistake I could ever make.

I want him to tell me everything is going to be okay, and for a second, I foolishly believe that he might. But instead, he retreats to the driver's side and punches a few buttons on his phone, pulling up a café on Google maps. A glance back at Archer ensures me that he doesn't suspect anything. He doesn't know how dangerous this man might possibly be.

We drive in silence, and I can't stop watching Conor, waiting for the bomb to drop. My anxiety is crawling through my veins like poison, and I don't know what to do.

"Ivy." Conor reaches over and squeezes my knee. "Quit staring. We'll talk about this later."

With some difficulty, I manage to redirect my attention to the road, and after a few minutes, Conor pulls into the café. He ushers us into the shop and directs us to sit down while he orders. Archer and I wait quietly before Conor returns with hot chocolates in hand.

"Here ye go, wee lad." He slides one over to Archer and then me.

"Be careful," I tell Archer. "That's hot."

"It's not too hot," Conor says. "I told them to make it just right."

I study him, wondering how he would even have the foresight to do something like that. "Do you have kids?"

"No." He doesn't look at me when he answers. "But I had a little brother to look out for."

There's a vulnerability in his voice that catches my attention, but I don't ask him to elaborate. Right now, my focus needs to be on surviving. Conor was following me for a reason, and there's only one reason that could be. He knows what I know, and I'm fucked.

I try not to think about it while we drink our hot chocolate and he tells jokes to Archer like it's completely natural to him. Like we aren't sitting at the table with a man who works for the Irish mob.

The trip back doesn't do anything to allay my fears either. I'm wound up so tight I can hardly breathe when he pulls into Lacey's driveway without even asking for directions. Further proof that he's been following me all morning. Possibly even longer than that.

"Time to say goodbye," Conor tells me. "Give the lad a kiss and a hug and send him inside."

I can't look at him or think about what those words might really mean. Instead, I take Archer inside and squeeze him like I've never hugged him before. And then I manage to make it all the way back to the car before I break down completely.

Eight

Conor

She starts sobbing the moment she gets back into the car, and I can't handle it.

"Jaysus." My fingers squeeze the life out of the steering wheel. "You have a fecking kid?"

"Please," she chokes out. "Please don't hurt him. He has nothing to do with this."

It isn't the bleeding kid I'm worried about. I can't even look at her, knowing that she's a mam. That changes things. It changes every goddamned thing.

When I saw her in that park with that little boy, I nearly lost my shite. He was so small. So innocent. All I could think of when I first saw him was Brady. I can still remember when he was that age, scared and alone in this world with only me to protect him.

And now I'm supposed to take away this kid's mammy? The tiny creature sitting next to me who couldn't hurt a fecking fly on her best day?

Ivy's voice rises to a crescendo as her panic grows, and she blurts out anything she thinks will save her. Promises to do whatever she's told. Working for free. Offers to give me anything I want. I glare at her, and she reaches out for me frantically, clinging to my jacket.

"I won't say anything, I swear it. I swear, Conor. I never saw anything."

"Don't—" I try to tell her to shut up because I don't want to hear what she's about to say. I don't want her to seal her fate. But Ivy is past the point of reason.

"I don't care. Honestly, I wanted him dead. You guys did me a favor. You freed me. I would never say a thing to anyone. I haven't so far, can't you see that?"

"For fucks sake," I growl. "Just stop talking before you condemn yourself any further."

Her tears continue in soft, silent sobs all the way back to Boston. And I can't think. I can't figure out how I'm supposed to sort her out. We end up back at my townhouse. I've never brought a woman here, and I don't know what I'm thinking doing it now.

Ivy sniffles as I drag her inside. "What are you going to do?"

I don't have an answer to that. Crow is counting on me, and he was right about her. But chrissakes if I want to kill a mam.

I haul her into my bedroom and point to the bed. "Sit."

Blonde strands of hair fly around her face as she shakes her head, arguing and carrying on all over again. I can't deal with this shite right now. I can't even look at her. And maybe it's cheap, but I'm not going to manhandle her, so I yank my Glock out from the back of my jeans and gesture to the bed again.

"Sit. The. Fuck. Down."

A flood of tears leak from her eyes, but this time, she doesn't hesitate to do as she's told.

"I'll do anything you want." She closes her eyes and bows her head. "All the cash I earn dancing, it's yours. I can clean your house. Cook. Whatever you want, Conor. Please…"

She looks up at me with a face so broken it physically hurts me to see her this way.

"I'll let you do whatever you want to me," she blurts. "Just give me your word that he'll be okay."

"Stop carrying on like that," I snarl. "Did I ask ye to spread your goddamn legs for me?"

She curls into a ball and sobs harder. "I don't know what you want. I'm desperate, can't you see that? I'll do anything! I don't care."

"Just stop fecking talking!" I edge my way toward the closet and rifle through the duffle bag I keep there. After a few minutes, I finally find what I'm looking for. Ivy freaks when I approach her with the rope, and this time, she tries to scramble for the end of the bed.

I catch her around the ankle and drag her back, climbing on top of her and using the weight of my body to pin her. It doesn't take much. She's only a wee thing, and I didn't think she had much fight in her, but she's wilder than I imagined. She bucks and screams and tries with all her might to wiggle from my grasp, and we're not getting anywhere like this.

"Ivy." My fingers clamp down around her jaw, forcing her to hold still and look at me. I brush the tangled mess of hair from her eyes, and when she looks up at me, chest heaving and lips wet, I freeze. An unbidden image of her lying naked beneath me comes to mind, and I have to shake myself out of it.

"It's okay," I force out roughly. "I'm just tying your wrists. Now be a good girl and hold still."

She squeezes her eyes shut and releases a shaky breath, and all I want to do is sample those salty tears on her lips. My fingers brush over her throat for no particular reason and she shivers. Her eyes are glassy and beautiful when they open to meet mine, and I don't know how the fuck she's doing this to me. She's poisoning me against everything I love, trying to take away my life. My brotherhood. And I can't look at her.

I force my gaze away and finish the task at hand, securing her wrists to the bed frame.

"Please look at me, Conor," she begs. "I'm human. A mother. A person. I got wrapped up in some bad shit, and that isn't my fault. I'll explain it all to you if you let me. I'll tell you everything, and then you'll understand."

"I don't want to understand." I finish off the knot and retreat from the bed. "That's what you don't get."

She curls into herself and I aim to put as much distance between us as I can while I figure out what the fuck I'm going to do.

I shut the door behind me and walk down the hall, taking up residence on my sofa. My eyes fall to the Glock in my hands, and an empty cavern opens up within my chest. Since my induction into the syndicate, I've never hesitated to kill anyone who was a threat to my brotherhood. But when I think about doing it now, it isn't what I want at all.

Heaviness settles into my limbs when I imagine her death. Seeing those pretty blue eyes so lifeless? I'll never get over that. I'll never find a way to make peace with this decision. But what choice do I have?

The hours tick by as I bounce from one conclusion to another, debating every possible alternative. But there are none. Every route is a dead end with the same conclusion. Crow asked this one thing of me. The only thing he's ever asked me to do in confidence. It's my chance to prove myself, show my loyalty. And if I don't do it, I'm fucked.

Ivy's fucked anyway. If it isn't me that kills her, somebody else will. At least I could make it easy on her. It doesn't have to be a bullet. There are a million other ways. Pills, for example. I could make it like she just fell asleep. But when I close my eyes and her face haunts my mind, I know that doesn't make a goddamn difference. She'll still be dead, and I'll still be the fucking piece of shite who did it.

I turn to my old friend Jameson to help me decide. Only, that just makes everything blurrier and less logical. I'm not any closer to a decision, but I am drunk when I wander back down the hall, Glock in hand.

Ivy is wide awake, curled into a ball, a trembling mess of nerves. She's afraid of me. And it isn't something I ever wanted to see in a woman's eyes. Her gaze is fixed on the weapon in my hand, chest heaving as she waits for me to use it on her.

"There's only one way to fix this mess," I slur.

I glance down at the pistol in my hand and disengage the magazine, and Ivy loses it, thrashing against the bed because she doesn't fucking get it. She doesn't get that she's ruined me. That she's probably going to get me killed.

I eject the cartridge and set the round on the nightstand, a physical reminder of what should have been. Ivy wheezes and peers up at me with the first sign of hope I've seen in her all day when I stuff the Glock back into my jeans.

"Like I said, there's only one way to fix this, but ye're not going to like it any better than I do."

"What is it?" she whispers.

"If ye fancy your life all that much, then ye're gonna have to marry me."

Nine

Ivy

"I can't marry you," I blurt, horrified.

Conor shoots me a withering glare and gestures to his gun. "Fine, have it your way then. Your kid can grow up without a mum."

My teeth grind together under the weight of his threat. "You don't have to be such an asshole. There has to be another way."

Conor paces the length of the room, his spine rigid. "What, do ye think ye're too good for me, is that it? Like I fecking want to marry you? A skinny ass crack addict."

"I'm not a fucking addict!" I shout. "I'm just hungry!"

For a split second, shame colors his eyes, and he looks away to hide it. "There isn't another way, Ivy. It's this or nothing. And even this is liable to earn me a bullet in the head if I'm lucky. I'm sticking me neck out for ye here, can ye not see that?"

My shoulders cave inward, and I feel so fucking empty. What he's saying is probably true, but that doesn't make it any easier to accept. They don't have any good reason to keep me around. In the end, my life means nothing to them. What Conor's offering me is the only solution in which I'll stay alive, but I'm supposed to get out of this city, and that plan doesn't include marrying into the mafia. If I had any tears left to cry, I would. But tears aren't going to get me anywhere.

I was foolish to believe they wouldn't find out about me. All I've managed to do was jump from the frying pan straight into the fire. And I hate Conor for even suggesting this stupid idea. For coming in here so casually and telling me in no uncertain terms that my life is over one way or the other. I can live in a prison of his making, or I can die. Those are my choices.

I'll never accept that this is going to be my life. But right now, I need to think short term. I learned from Muerto that sometimes just buying myself another day on this earth is all that matters. It isn't even about me anymore. It's about Archer and doing whatever I can to ensure that I'm in his life. He is the only deciding factor at stake.

"Okay." It physically hurts to speak, but I force the words out. "If we do this, can you guarantee that Archer will be safe? That you will never let any harm come to him?"

Conor meets my eyes, and even though he can be a prick, there's a softness to him when it comes to my son. "Ye have my word. I will look out for the kid. On my life, no harm will ever come to him."

All the air deflates from my lungs and I slump forward as I utter the last thing I ever thought I'd say. "Then I guess we should probably get married."

Conor unties me from the bed, and then he tells me not to get any bright ideas about trying to run before he stumbles back down the hall to the living room. I opt to stay in his bedroom while he sobers up, keeping as much distance between us as possible.

Conor's room is bare, but tidy. There aren't a lot of personal effects in here, which I discover when I peek into the closet and a couple of his drawers. There's a bed, clothes, and some ammo. But in the nightstand, I find one photo. It's of Conor and another boy, taken when he was much younger. I can only assume it must be his brother, since the resemblance is so striking. They both have the same vivid green eyes and the same mischievous smile. A smile I've never seen in person. I don't know if the man is even capable of such a thing anymore.

It leaves me with more questions than answers about him. Why doesn't he have any photos of the rest of his family? What happened to his brother? And why is he so hell bent that I must be a drug addict?

I put the photo away and use the next hour to scribble my thoughts into my journal. It's a small, pocket sized notebook I can carry in my coat, and for the last year, it's been my only real outlet.

When Muerto stole my life, everything I had was left behind. All my memories. All the personal things that make a house a home. I don't even know what happened to them, but they're just… gone. Every day, I'm left to consider what would have happened to my son if I hadn't taken him to Lacey's in time. It isn't something I like to think about because when I think about it, I get angry, and now it feels like history is repeating itself all over again.

It might not be logical, but all those hateful thoughts spill over into my journal, attaching themselves to Conor's name. I hate him for doing this to me. I hate him and his asshole mafia for fucking up my life and taking away my control. The only weapon I have left is my pen, and I use it to my fullest advantage, scribbling every acidic thought I have until I feel better.

And it does make me feel better. Conor's trying to paint himself as the hero in this situation. Telling me he's putting his life on the line, sticking his neck out for me. But he has other choices, even if he doesn't want to admit it. He could have sent me away. He could have let me go. If I can hide from the Locos, surely, I could hide from his mafia too.

At least for a little while.

It does me no good to dwell on it. Right now, I don't know how I'm going to get myself out of this mess, but I will get out of it. It's the only belief I can grab onto. The bigger picture is all that matters and in the interim, I will take everything in baby steps. Today, I will be grateful that I'm alive. That Archer is safe. And tomorrow, if I have to marry Conor to survive another week on this earth, then that's what I will do. The road to my freedom is paved with patience.

Freaking out and spewing hate at Conor isn't going to help this situation. I need to play nice and break down his barriers. I need to figure out how this situation is going to work so that I can manipulate it in my favor, and I need to start now.

So, after spending three hours alone in the bedroom, I finally work up the courage to walk down the hall. Conor's house is the typical bachelor pad. From my small exploration I conclude there are two bedrooms and a bathroom and nothing homey about the place. Everything he owns is for function only, and there isn't a single decorative piece in sight.

I find the man himself on the couch, nursing a cup of coffee and what looks like a wicked hangover. It's not even five o'clock yet. I sit down on a chair opposite him and he glares at me like he wishes I would just drop dead. It's obvious he isn't happy about this either, so what I really want to ask is why he's doing it at all. He must be getting something out of it, but what that might be I can't imagine.

The tension between us is awkward, and after five minutes of not speaking, I can't handle it anymore. "Do you want some lunch? It might help with the hangover."

Conor looks at his watch with bleary eyes. "Christ, when's the last time ye ate yourself?"

"I ate one of the donuts you gave me this morning."

He shakes his head, almost like he's disappointed with himself, but I can't be sure. "You need to eat. There's some makings for a sandwich in the fridge, but not much else."

"I'll make a couple of them," I volunteer.

He doesn't argue. Five minutes later, we're sitting at the table together in more awkward silence. I can feel his eyes on me while I eat, so I attempt to slow down and act like this isn't one of the most delicious meals I've had in a week.

"Those things I said about you being an addict," he mutters. "If it's true that ye're just hungry, then it was a shitty thing for me to say."

I look up at him, and my heart feels funny. Is he apologizing? Just when I think he actually means it, he has to go and ruin it.

"But just so ye know, if the opposite is true, it's going to be finished here and now. No wife of mine will be on drugs. I don't care if I have to chain ye to the bed and—"

"I'm not a fucking addict," I snap. "What is with you and that word? You toss it around more often than you breathe. Haven't you ever heard not to judge a book by the cover?"

He looks away to hide something in his eyes, but I can't help noticing how rigid his shoulders have gone. There's something behind that tension, a story. A raw wound. And I intend to get to the bottom of it eventually, but for now, I need to establish this one thing with him.

"If this is going to work, you'll need to trust me, right? So, for starters, how about we stop beating this dead horse and you just listen to me. I've never touched an illegal drug in my life, and that includes marijuana."

Conor looks up at me again, his eyes unconvinced, but I could swear I see hope there too.

My voice softens, and I feel compelled to go on. "Despite what you might think, I'm a good person. I've only ever tried to live a straight life, but things just got fucked up along the way."

"How so?" he asks.

I fidget with the napkin in my lap as I debate how much I should tell him. "I didn't go looking for trouble. It found me."

Conor finishes up his sandwich and pushes the empty plate away. "You mean Muerto?"

"Yes, that's exactly what I mean."

He leans back in his chair and studies me. "I'll need to know what happened. Crow will want the details when it comes down to it, so you might as well tell me."

That sounds like a bullshit excuse because he doesn't want to admit he's curious himself. But regardless, I indulge him.

"I was never Muerto's girlfriend," I begin. "I was his captive."

The muscles in Conor's forearms flex as he folds his hands together, and I can tell he's skeptical, but I don't really care. This story has been bottled up inside for so long, it's long overdue to be uncorked.

"Archer's dad was in the military," I tell him. "An old school friend that I hooked up with once when he was home on leave. We weren't together, and I didn't even know how to get in touch with him when he left. He died in combat before I could even tell him I was pregnant, so all the responsibility fell on me."

Conor's brows pinch together, and for a second, something softens in him. Something that makes me believe he can relate and gives me the courage to go on.

"I was a hairstylist," I explain. "And I had a booth in a salon, but it was expensive to maintain. Being that I had a kid to look after on my own, I had to take a second job helping at a barber shop as the shampoo girl. It wasn't glamorous, but it supplemented my income. I was making it work. But then one night Muerto decided to come in for a haircut."

My fingers twist under the table as I recall that first time I saw him. Right away, my gut told me it was bad. The way he looked at me, I'll never forget it. His eyes were soulless, a shade of black I'd never even seen until then.

"He wasn't the kind of guy to ask a girl on a date," I rattle. "The Locos had a mantra that I came to know well. *Mata. Viola. Controla.* It means kill, rape, control. From the second he walked into that shop, I was fucked."

"What did he do?" Conor demands.

I stare down at the pale, cold fingers in my lap. "He stalked me. Harassed me. Told me I would be his whether I liked it or not. I was terrified, and I went to the cops. They said I could get a restraining order, but it would be difficult to prove. Somehow, Muerto found out and he went ballistic. When I went into work the next night, the shop was closed, and the owner was dead. Muerto's crew had murdered him to send me a message."

My throat clogs with emotion as I meet Conor's eyes. "He had two young children and they just killed him like it was nothing. When I got home, there was a guy at my door. His friend Animal came to tell me that if I thought about going to the cops again, my son would be next. He knew where I lived, where I worked. He knew everything about my life. I didn't have the money to run. I had no-where to go without getting someone else killed. My only option was to get Archer out of there, so at least he would be safe. I took him to Lacey, and it was only supposed to be for a couple weeks."

"In my mind, I became resigned to the fact that he was going to fuck me, one way or another. I hoped it would be once and he'd get it out of his system. But the first night he took me in an alley on my way home from work, he told me he wasn't letting me go, and he meant it. He took me to their compound and locked me up in that room. For an entire year, I didn't see the sun. I was left there to rot, only useful when he decided he wanted to toy with me. He fucked with my head, threatened my son, starved and beat me because it was a game to him."

A tear splashes against my plate, and I realize that I'm crying again. It's humiliating how much I've cried in front of Conor already, but when I look up at him, there is no more judgment in his eyes. All that's left now is rage.

"I would kill that motherfucker," he growls. "If he were still here, I would have made him pay for ye, Ivy."

I shake my head. "It doesn't matter. He's gone, and I'm out. I get to see Archer now. That's what I have to focus on."

"What about the others?" Conor presses. "Did they ever touch ye?"

"Not if they wanted to live," I laugh dryly. "Muerto didn't share me. But I'm fair game now that's he's dead. That's why I can't let them catch me."

"You won't ever have to worry about that," Conor assures me. "Those shitebags won't live long enough to touch ye again. I'll make sure of that."

Ten

Conor

Ivy's been in the bathroom for over a bleeding hour, and I can't figure out what she's doing in there. The whiskey has leached from my system, but I'm bristling with an edge I haven't felt since Brady's death. I want to go kill every one of those Loco fuckers and string their bodies from the streetlights in downtown Boston as a warning to anyone else who thinks about fecking with a woman.

I make a mental note to speak to Dom so I can thank him for killing that scumbag Muerto and ask him if he suffered. I need the details. It's the only way I can feel any peace after Ivy told me her story. I already feel like a big enough shitebag as it is, accusing her of being a street rat and a drug whore.

I have every intention of making some sort of amends, but when she comes down the hall with her hair and makeup all done up, that notion goes right out the window. My cock springs to attention as my eyes drift over her body. Even when she had nothing but a plain face and shabby clothes on, I couldn't deny she was beautiful. But now she's clean and smells like vanilla and her eyes are all smoky, it's a different fucking animal. I don't know what the hell she thinks she's doing.

"What's the craic with that getup?" I ask.

She chews on her lip and glances down at herself. "I have to go to work, remember?"

Christ. She's right. Crow's expecting her.

"He gave ye the night off," I lie.

I'll deal with Crow later. I don't know why it fecking matters, but I don't want her dancing tonight. Not after all the things she told me this afternoon.

She frowns. "Why would he do that? Did he not like my work?"

"It isn't that." I tear my eyes away from hers. "It's just a scheduling mishap."

I feel like an arsehole for lying to her, even though I shouldn't. If I'm going to make the best of this situation, I need to remember that her feelings aren't important. That's the only way we can make this work. It needs to be a business arrangement. That's what I try to remember as I catch my gaze roaming the subtle curves of her body again.

"You can make yourself at home in my room," I grunt. "I haven't done much with the spare room yet."

"What about you?" she asks.

"I don't often make it past the couch. I won't be bothering you."

She seems to consider this for a minute, and she still isn't getting how bad I just need her out of my sight right now before I do something stupid.

"You'll probably want an early night," I add. "We have a big day tomorrow."

"What's happening tomorrow?" She frowns.

My jaw grinds down so hard I can barely get the words out. "We're getting married."

Eleven

Ivy

When I wake up in Conor's bed, it almost seems surreal how much my life has changed in the matter of twenty-four hours. I went from sleeping behind a dumpster to a warm bed, and after today, I'll be married.

I spend an hour scribbling in my journal, thinking that if I can somehow see my thoughts written in ink, it will make me feel better about the situation. But it doesn't take the edge off. Not this time.

When I finally manage to swallow down my nerves and face the day, I find Conor sitting at the kitchen table with two fresh cups of Dunkie's coffee and more donuts. He wasn't kidding when he said that's what they usually get.

"Good morning." I sit down across from him.

His attention flicks from his phone to me, and I wonder if he's even aware that his eyes are wandering over my body again. From the first time he opened his mouth, I was dead sure he didn't find me attractive. In fact, he made a point of letting me know it, several times. Other than the slight sting his words left behind, I was okay with that. After Muerto, I couldn't imagine I would ever want a man's attention again.

But right now, with Conor's eyes on me, something feels different. My stomach is all fluttery and my cheeks feel too warm, and maybe there's a small part of me that does like it. Maybe there's even a small part of me that wants it, as crazy as that might be. And it is crazy. So crazy that I need to bleach those thoughts from my mind before they can leave a stain.

"Morning," he says gruffly. "I sorted ye some breakfast. There's a couple sandwiches in that bag if ye don't fancy another donut."

"Thanks." I take a coffee and another donut while he returns to his phone, tapping text messages. When I finish my breakfast in silence, Conor points to the couch without looking at me.

"There are clothes too. At least a few warmer things for now. We can sort ye out a real shopping trip later."

I glance at the pile of bags on the couch, and my body stills. The gesture is completely unexpected, and immediately I'm wondering what strings are attached. I'm not in the habit of accepting handouts from people, especially if they come with baggage.

Conor glances at me and shakes his head. "I don't expect anything in return, Ivy. They're just clothes."

I feel like an idiot for even thinking otherwise. Especially when I tried to fling myself at him any which way I could offer last night in a bid to protect Archer. He didn't accept then, so I don't know why he would now.

I pad over to the sofa and examine the pieces he bought me. There's a winter coat and a couple lighter jackets. In another bag, I find all the cold weather basics. Scarves, beanies, gloves, jeans, boots, and sweaters. And a multi pack of cotton underwear, along with two bras.

"How did you know what sizes to get?"

A flush creeps over Conor's face as he shifts in the chair. "I looked through your bag."

Heat pricks at my neck, and I want to be angry at him for invading my privacy, but how can I? It was a nice gesture, or at least it seems like it. Even if it makes me feel slightly humiliated that he had to buy me clothes at all, it doesn't feel like that was his intention.

"Is there a problem?" he asks.

"No." I clear my throat. "I'm just... these are really nice. Thank you."

"I didn't pick them out," he says. "So, I can't take credit for that. Crow's wife did all the shopping."

"Then I should probably thank her too." I go about the business of picking out something to wear for the day before Conor stops me.

"There's a dress in the bathroom."

"A dress?"

"Aye," he grunts. "For the ceremony."

Right. *We're getting married today.* And he bought me a dress. My heart is beating so hard it feels like it's going to blow out of my chest. "Where are we doing it?"

The words come out all wrong, and my cheeks heat when Conor turns to me with a smirk. "We'll exchange vows at City Hall. Nothing too fancy. But ye should at least have a dress."

I stare down at my toes. "Are you sure you want to do this? You could just send me away, you know. Archer and I can disappear, and I wouldn't be a hindrance in your life. You wouldn't have to change anything."

The muscle in his jaw tenses, and his eyes darken. "No can do. You've seen some shite ye were never meant to see and this is the only way I can keep you and my crew safe."

There's no point arguing. Conor has made up his mind, and I won't be changing it. But I still can't help wondering if he really knows what he's getting himself into.

"So, it's just the two of us then?" I ask, for no other reason than to break the awkward silence that lingers between us as we wait in the hall.

Conor tugs at the tie around his neck like it's strangling him. "I'll tell Crow after."

He looks as sick about the thought as I currently feel. My blood is pumping so hard and fast it sounds like a freight train running through my ears. I'm lightheaded and nauseous and I can't stop glancing at the exit, wondering if I could actually make it. But then, out of nowhere, Conor takes my hand in his to stop me from shaking.

"It will all work out. No sense letting yourself get out of sorts over it."

He sounds so certain, but how can he be? I search his eyes and as tense as he might be, all I find there is calm. So much calm. I don't know how he can be so okay with this. Signing his life over to someone he barely knows. But then again, I guess it doesn't really work that way in the mafia. If he gets sick of me, he can just get rid of me. I'm pretty sure I don't have the same option. But I will be his wife. A role that I'm certain comes with expectations. It's enough to make any sane person fall off the deep end. But when I look at Conor, steady and strong and fearless, I have to believe that it will be okay. What choice do I have? I'm in it now. At least for the time being.

I study the lines of his face. The long lashes and angular jaw and those soulful green eyes. He is handsome in an obvious way, but there are so many subtleties I have yet to unearth. With our eyes locked on each other, it occurs to me that I want to know them. Like that scar above his eyebrow, how did he get it? Or the callouses on his hands… what made him so hard? I want to know his secrets. The things that hurt him. The things that shaped who he is today. These are dangerous thoughts to have. I'm not supposed to care, and I try to remind myself of that when he squeezes my hand and they call our names.

We follow the clerk into a small room set up with a few chairs and the officiant who is already waiting. The walk up the aisle is entirely too short, and I still don't know if I can do this. But then I catch sight of our reflection in the mirror on the wall in front of us. Conor in his white button-down shirt and black vest, and me in the white lace dress he picked out for me.

It isn't a traditional wedding by any means, but you wouldn't know that by looking at us. From the outside, we look like any other bride and groom about to take the plunge. A little nervous, a lot flushed. But there's one thing about this picture I can't deny.

Conor hasn't taken his eyes off me. And when the vows are read, he repeats them back word for word like they really mean something to him. It scares me even more than the idea that they don't. Nevertheless, I find myself caught up in the moment, repeating them back just the same.

The ceremony is short, simple, and to the point. It's over before I can really grasp what I've done. And then the officiant pronounces us husband and wife.

Mr. and Mrs. O'Callahan.

She tells Conor he can kiss me, and nervous laughter bubbles up my throat but gets caught there before it can escape. He's staring at me like he didn't think about this part. I'm trying to think of something to say, but Conor surprises me when he steps forward and slides his hand up to rest on the back of my neck.

"Just a wee one," he whispers. And then his head tilts toward mine, hot lips brushing against my mouth that currently feels like the desert.

I'm too stunned to think about it. I can't understand what's happening when Conor lets out the smallest of groans, and I start to kiss him back. My lips part, and his tongue invades my mouth as his grip on me tightens. My head spins, and I feel off balance, almost drunk as I melt into his body. He's so bad for me, but nothing else has ever felt so good.

He tastes of whiskey and mint and danger. *So much danger.* Surely, I should remember that. But I can't seem to think of anything else when my hands curl into his vest, adhering to him as our simple kiss turns into an almost x rated show for the officiant.

Conor is the one who finally pulls away, breathless and stunned as his brows pinch together and he examines me like he doesn't know what just happened either. Neither of us acknowledges it as we put ourselves back together and look anywhere but at each other.

At Conor's request, the clerk snaps a few perfunctory photos of us, and then we are free to leave. Or in their words, free to start our lives of wedded bliss together.

Twelve

Conor

Outside City Hall, the rest of the bleeding world carries on with their lives as if they don't have a clue how badly I've just fucked up mine. I offer Ivy a smile for her benefit, but she doesn't notice. As soon as we stepped outside, she shut down, opting for despondency as we drive in silence.

I want to assure her again that everything is going to be alright, but I can't find it in me to do it. Telling Crow that I've gone behind his back and married the girl I was supposed to kill is not a recipe for good things to come.

The enormity of what I've done hits me in waves. I don't suspect Ivy is all that clued in on our mafia culture, and I probably should have warned her that when we marry, that contract lasts a lifetime. It doesn't matter if she hates the sight of me, we signed our names on the dotted line and now she's mine and I'm hers. *Forever.*

When I sneak a glance at her, pale and uncertain, it occurs to me that I like the idea of that a little too much. As fecked up as the whole situation might be, the man in me is satisfied with the fact that I've laid claim to her. At least, in my own mind. It will take some time before I confess to Crow. I need to let him get used to the idea before I drop a bomb like this.

There are rules we all have to abide by. And if there's one thing I can be certain of, it's that I've saved Ivy's life and secured her protection from the brotherhood.

Wives are off limits.

Maybe it's cheap, but Crow will have to honor that sacred agreement. It doesn't mean he can't and won't have me killed for it though. What I've done is a betrayal of our trust, and I'll remember that every time I look myself in the mirror.

I never thought there was anything that could test my loyalty. Two weeks ago, nothing could have convinced me otherwise. But two weeks ago, I didn't know her. There is something about this girl that crawled under my skin the moment she stumbled into my life. It was easy to believe that I did all of this because of the kid. I didn't want him growing up an orphan. But that has nothing to do with the way my eyes have been roaming over her. Or the fact that when we kissed it was like ten thousand volts of electricity straight to my dick. Now all I can seem to think about is being inside of her. Owning her. Laying claim to her body and her mind.

Ivy doesn't seem to be on the same train of thought. Her hands curl together in her lap all the way home and she stares out the window, silent. I want to know what she's thinking. I want to know what she's feeling, and I hate myself for it.

If this is going to work, I need to cop on to myself. Ivy isn't here because she likes me. She isn't here because she wants me. She's here because it's the only way she can stay alive. At the end of the day, there will always be a part of her that hates me.

The reality of our situation makes my throat itch for a drink and my fists desperate to pummel a punching bag just to bleed some of this tension out of my body. But before I do any of that I have to establish the ground rules with her.

The moment we walk in the door, she tries to make a mad dash down the hall to change out of her dress, and I grab her by the arm. She looks up at me, wide eyed, pink cheeks, and so pretty I could fuck her right now. I wonder if she's thought about it. I wonder if the idea repulses her. And then I wonder what the fuck is wrong with me.

I tell her to sit down on the couch and she does. My eyes rake over her, and she's back to being skittish as a fecking mouse. We have a long way to go. She's been beaten down by life and hungry for far too long and I intend to put a good twenty pounds back on her frame by feeding her regular meals and taking care of her. But the first thing I need to do is establish how this relationship is going to work between us.

"I have to go out tonight," I tell her. "Work shite. But before you go getting any big ideas about running out on me, I need you to know one thing. If ye do run there isn't a place on this earth I won't find you. That my brothers won't find you. And those vows we said today, I meant them, Ivy. I hope you took them seriously, because I won't be able to save you if you break them. I know what Muerto did to you. I know the threats he made. But ye have my word as long as there's breath in my lungs Archer will be safe. I can't promise you the same unless you stay here and abide by my rules."

Her eyes are glassy, but she jerks her chin in agreement. I'm fairly certain I've made my point when she comes back at me with something I seem to have forgotten.

"I still have to work tonight," she says. "Crow is expecting me, and I can't let him down."

Her observation feeds the irritation festering inside of me. She's right that Crow's expecting her, but that isn't what bothers me. What bothers me is that she wants to go. It shouldn't make a damn bit of difference to me. I have no reason to deny her being up on that stage for all the world to see. Other than the fact that she's now my wife, and I don't want any other bleeding imbeciles looking at her like that. But I'm not about to admit that to her especially when I don't want her getting any ideas that this is any sort of romantic arrangement between us.

Ivy holds her breath and waits for me to tell her what we're going to do.

"I still want to work," she volunteers. "I can't just sit around here with nothing to do, and I gave Crow my word."

I want to prove it makes no goddamned difference to me, and that's the reason I find myself nodding along. But I can't change the fact that my voice is full of acid. "If shaking your arse up on stage for all the lads to see is what gets your jollies off, be my guest. You better sort yourself out because I'm heading to the club in ten minutes."

And with that sentiment I leave her on the couch while I fuck on out the door to wait in the car.

Thirteen

Ivy

Conor's knuckles are white as he drives to the club, and any connection we might have shared earlier is gone now. Tension bleeds into his body with every second we spend together, and I don't feel like I can breathe again until we finally pull into the parking lot of Sláinte and open the doors.

We are both absent of words as we walk inside together, and when I look at him, he refuses to return the gesture. Instead, he disappears into the void of the club while I stand there feeling wrung out and confused.

"There ye are." Crow appears out of nowhere, scaring the hell out of me. He looks at me expectantly, and I swallow hard, wondering what it is he wants. I can barely look at him because I'm certain he'll be able to figure out what we did.

"Feeling better?" he asks.

I stare blankly, uncertain what he means. He seems annoyed with me when I don't respond and looks at me as if I can't comprehend basic English.

"Conor said ye had one hell of a bug." He arches a brow. "I just need to be sure ye aren't getting the other girls sick if that's the case."

My mouth feels like sandpaper as I process his words. Conor told me Crow gave me the night off last night, but obviously that was a bullshit lie. What I can't figure out is why he would say that. But the last thing I want to do is give Crow any more doubts about my character. If Conor told him I was sick, then I was sick.

"I'm much better." I force a smile. "It was just a quick bug."

Crow crosses his arms and shakes his head. "I have to tell ye, so far ye aren't making a real big impression on me. Ye beg me for the job and then call in sick the second day. I hope this isn't going to be a regular occurrence."

"It won't," I promise.

"Alright then, I'll leave ye to it. Ye're on in twenty, so best be getting ready. And for the record, ye need to be here a little earlier so you can give yourself time to prepare."

He retreats down the hall and I gulp in a few large breaths as I venture in the direction of the dressing rooms. I hate this constant edginess inside me and I wonder if it will ever go away.

I attempt to focus on the task of getting ready, but I'm even more of a mess than usual. It's been a crazy day. One surreal event after another. This afternoon, I got married. And now, I'm at a strip club getting ready to take off my clothes for the world to see. Not exactly a fairytale ending.

Tears prick my eyes, and I wave my hands in front of my face, hoping they don't ruin my makeup. I told myself I could do this. I told myself that I could dance naked as long as it put some desperately needed cash in my pocket. I swore that I would do anything to earn money if it meant getting Archer out of this city safely.

The first time I danced, I was so high on adrenaline and the simple prospect of a job, it seemed like I could do anything. But now

I'm keenly aware that I'm married to one of these guys. A truth that's going to come out sooner or later. And when it does, all his friends will have seen me naked. It makes my stomach flip. It makes me want to vomit.

The fact that Conor lied to keep me away from here keeps playing on repeat through my mind. There must have been a reason. He must have felt the same way too. That's the only plausible explanation for his surly behavior the entire way over. But if he didn't want me dancing tonight, he didn't say so. Not in words, anyway.

It's not like it matters. Regardless of what happened today, I need this job and the money it brings in. I have to go out on that stage and shake my ass and forget about the fact that I have a warm home and food in my belly for now. In the grand scheme of things, this situation is only temporary. My longevity lies in making money and planning my escape.

With that thought at the forefront of my mind, I force one platformed heel in front of the other when my name is called. But I'm totally off my game tonight, and I don't feel sexy at all. I'm too stiff and trying to dance organically isn't working. Even if I somehow manage to make it through the whole set, Crow will probably fire me for scaring customers away.

The intro is long, but the first two minutes pass in a blur of uncoordinated chaos. The intensity of the stage lights makes it difficult, but I can still make out Conor's form in the back watching me from the shadows. I wish that I could see his face while the other men chant for me to take it all off.

The worst thing is there's a part of me that wishes he would save me from this too. It's silly and stupid and entirely impractical to want for such things. He isn't my prince charming and I can't allow hope to bloom where none exists. I'm nothing to Conor. We are married in name only, and he won't hesitate to kill me just like he threatened if I step outside of the invisible boundaries.

My throat works to hold back too many emotions as I untie the strings of my bikini top. The crowd gets louder as they shout encouragement, and the shadow I was focused on has disappeared into the fray. I'm on my own now. As alone as I've ever been.

I focus on Archer and the dream I've always had. Just me, and him, and the cape. Someday, this will be a distant memory while we build sandcastles by the sea. That's what I tell myself as I allow my top to drop to the floor beneath me.

My stomach is a riot of nerves, and then without warning, there's a riot around me. Someone shouts something and the music stutters before two huge hands grab me from behind and yank me back into the shadows, tossing a coat over my body.

"Conor?" I blink.

"For fucks sake." He stares at me like he doesn't know what he's doing either. "This is over. I won't have my wife making a mockery of herself up on stage like this. It's done."

Before I have a chance to answer, our night gets a whole lot worse. Because now Crow is here, stage side, looking up at Conor like he's lost his fucking mind.

"Would ye care to tell me what the bleeding hell is going on here?"

Fourteen

Conor

We follow Crow down the hall and into his office where he tells some of the other lads to get the feck out. They offer me a pitiful look before they scramble, and Crow instructs me to take a seat across from his desk before turning to Ivy. "You can wait in the hall."

"No." I look him dead in the eye. "She stays in here with me."

He stares at me like I've gone mad, and I suppose I have, talking to him that way. But I don't trust having Ivy out of my sight for a second right now. I need his word that no harm will come to her, and in the meantime, I need her where I can see her, so she doesn't try to run off on me.

"Chrissakes." Crow yanks another chair out and gestures for her to sit down too. "By all means, don't listen to me."

He slams the office door shut and pours himself two fingers of whiskey. "What have ye done, Conor? Just fucking spit it out. I already know I'm not going to like it."

The disappointment on his face is worse than the possibility of confronting my own death. I hate that I've gone and trampled all over his trust. If it weren't for Crow, I wouldn't have anything. I've thrown it all away for a woman. But when I look at her, hands trembling in her lap while my jacket practically swallows her whole, I know I'd do it all over again. And Crow might say otherwise, but he would too.

"The thing is, I know what ye asked me to do," I tell him. "And I had every intention of following through on that. But there was a complication."

Crow narrows his eyes. "What sort of complication?"

"She has a son. A wee one. And she's the only parent he has left."

Ivy shoots me a look like I've just betrayed her, but she doesn't get how this works. This syndicate is a family, and we protect our own. Especially the wee ones. Family is something Crow understands, and I recognize that when he drains his glass in a hurry.

"Fecking Christ. Goddammit motherfucking—"

Ivy flinches as he begins to pace around the room. She's jumpy around him for good reason. I just can't figure out why she isn't like that with me. Crow glances at her and for a split second, he looks sorry for scaring her. But Crow isn't one to let his emotions get in the way of what's best for the brotherhood.

"Tell me what ye know." He points at her. "Whatever it is you saw, and don't leave anything out."

Ivy chews on her lip and looks to me for reassurance. I won't have her lie to Crow. There's no sense in that. I signal for her to go ahead, and she jerks her attention back to him.

"I was in the house that night your guys came. When the shots started, I hid in the closet. I didn't see anything, but I heard it. All I know is that when I finally came out, Muerto was dead."

The vein in Crow's neck pulses. "Conor, I'm going to need a word with ye in private now."

"It was the best day of my life—" Ivy blurts.

Crow cocks his head to the side and studies her carefully, looking for any sign of weakness or dishonesty.

"I know that sounds crazy," she admits. "But it really was. If it weren't for your guys killing Muerto, I would still be there. I would still be his prisoner."

Crow glances at me for confirmation. "It's true. She told me her story."

"And you believe her?" His voice is caustic.

"Aye," I growl. "I do. Kind of like you believed your wife back when you were in a situation not so different."

His mouth pinches into a hard line, and I know I shouldn't have brought it up. But he shouldn't have accused me of being ignorant when it comes to Ivy.

"What exactly are ye getting at, Conor?"

"I'm just reminding ye that we've all done things that don't necessarily fall in line. I know what ye asked me to do, and I had every intention of proving myself, since it seems like I never get the bloody chance. This was it for me. And you aren't going to like what I have to say, but I'm going to say it anyway."

He takes up the seat behind his desk again, and if I didn't know any better, he almost looks amused with this shite. "By all means, if ye have a point to make, then get to it."

I look to Ivy, and to drive it home, I reach for her hand. She takes mine without hesitation, and warmth fills the space between her fragile fingers in mine. Crow's eyes flick between us, searching for the answer I have yet to give him.

"I haven't got the rings yet, but it's legal."

"Fack off with this shite, Conor," Crow bites out. "You've got to be joking me. Don't tell me ye actually went and married her."

My hand tightens around hers. "Aye, I did. She's my wife now, and according to our laws, that means none of the brothers can touch her."

There's a full minute of silence in which Crow doesn't move or speak. He just sits there, staring at the both of us like he's trying to sort out who to murder first.

"What do you make of this?" he asks Ivy.

The question comes out of left field, and it's something I didn't prepare her for. I have no bleeding idea what she's going to say, but I'm almost dead certain it won't be anything good.

Ivy squares her posture and looks him straight in the eye. "I know what you wanted him to do, but you can't fault him for having a heart. He's given me the chance to let my son grow up with a mother. He's a good man. An honest man. And I think that he saved my life."

My eyes drift over her, drinking in the details of her face. I'm looking for the lies in her words, but I can't find them. She's vulnerable, but not as delicate as I thought. Her honesty comes off as genuine, and surely Crow will recognize that too.

Crow pours himself another drink and swirls the amber whiskey around his glass. "Ivy, I need ye to do me a wee favor now then. I need ye to wait up at the bar for Conor."

Our eyes meet, it looks like she's actually worried about me. But I rationalize it's more likely she's only worried what will happen to her if Crow decides to off me tonight.

"I'll be out shortly." I squeeze her hand. "It's okay."

She wraps my coat around her like a security blanket before she takes her leave, allowing Crow to speak his piece.

"You went against a direct order," he barks. "And ye have it in your thick head that you can just come in here and tell me that it's all sorted?"

"That isn't what I said. I know there are other details we need to work out, and ye have every right to throttle me for what I did. If that's your wish, then I don't need to grant ye my permission. My loyalty is to the brotherhood, let there be no bones about that. But I can't stand for an innocent woman and child to suffer just to save our necks. This was the only way I saw fit. And I know ye must be able to understand that, given the past history ye have with Mack."

"Quit bringing up my goddamn wife," he says. "She's got nothing to do with this. That was different."

"How?" I ask.

"Because I cared about her." He slams his glass down on the desk. "You barely know this girl. And now ye've just gone and saddled yourself to her for life. Have ye even considered that?"

"I know enough. She's had a rough go of it and she deserves a chance. I don't have any regrets over my decision."

Crow stares at me, dumbfounded. I'm fairly certain there's only one conclusion here. He's going to tell me to get my arse down to the basement, so he can break my leg or cut off a finger or something equally gruesome to dole out the punishment I deserve. But instead, he just sighs.

"Let us be clear about one thing," he says. "I'm not going soft in me ways. But I've watched you struggle to prove yourself to this syndicate from the day ye came stumbling into it. And if there's anything I can say about this bombshell ye just dropped on me, it's that I think ye finally have."

His words take me by surprise, and so does the laughter that spews from his chest. "Ye must really have a pair on you to walk in here tonight like ye did and state your case. You've come a long way from the young lad I first met. And for that, I'm proud of ye, Conor. But let's not make it a fecking habit, aye?"

"I've no intentions of disobeying ye again, Crow. Ye have my word on that."

"Grand," he answers. "Because now I have another task that will put that to the test."

"What is it?"

"You and Ivy need to keep this on the downlow for a while. Just a month or so. Let the lads see ye together and know ye're a couple before ye go dropping the big news that you've signed your life away to this girl. Otherwise, it will raise questions and set precedent for the other lads to go marrying whoever they fancy when the situation warrants it."

"It will remain quiet," I assure him.

Crow nods. "Don't think that just because you've put a ring on her finger, it's over. She's protected as long as she's worth protecting. It's up to you to keep her in line, now and forever. I expect ye to make a real go at it. Give her a life that she would die for, a husband she's proud to call hers. And down the line, get her in a family way."

The image of Ivy with a belly full of my child springs to mind, and my dick swells unexpectedly at the thought.

Crow smirks like he knows exactly what I'm thinking, and then he gestures for the door. "Now get the feck out of my office. I've got shite to do."

Fifteen

Conor

I chucked in the end, just as Reaper predicted.

It wasn't Albie's expressionless eyes or the gaping mouth where his tongue used to be. It was after Reaper got rid of the body, when I looked around the room, there was blood everywhere. And without the task of sawing off appendages and torture to distract me, I could smell it everywhere too. The metallic tang so thick on your lips you can taste it.

"Let's get ye cleaned up a wee bit," Crow says. "We'll sort ye out a lap dance before you come back down."

"Thanks," I mutter. "But I have a girlfriend."

He gives me an odd look, almost like he doesn't believe me. "Well she's not here now, is she? And ye don't seem all that concerned about her grieving over your loss."

His words hit me hard, but I don't bother mentioning that my girlfriend overdosed last month, right after she finished fucking her dealer. "I'd rather just get on with it," I say. "If you don't mind."

Before Crow can agree, Rory appears at the bottom of the steps with an older man in tow. Crow's face turns to stone when he spots the man, but he dips his head as a sign of respect. "Niall."

"Lachlan."

There's a long pause of silence as all three men look at each other, and then Niall turns his attention to me.

"This the lad?" he asks Rory.

"Aye, it is," Rory answers. "This is the young lad."

Crow's fists curl at his sides and he blows out a breath. "The lad made a deal. He knew what he was getting himself into, young or not."

"This true?" Niall looks to me. He's an older man, and by the way they wait for him to speak, I'm guessing he's the one in charge.

And now Crow's eyeballing me like he half expects me to be a snake. To rat him out or change my story.

"It's true," I say. "He gave me what I asked for, and I'm ready to fulfill my side of the deal."

Niall doesn't respond right away, and they are all quiet while he seems to sort the situation out in his head. "What's your name, laddy?"

"Conor O' Callahan," I answer.

"O' Callahan," Niall repeats quietly.

"Irish as the day is long," Rory says proudly.

Crow shakes his head. "Irish or not, we made a deal. The lad accepted it."

"Enough." Niall stuffs his hands into his coat pockets and turns to Crow. "Tell me why ye decided this was the best way to sort this out, Lachlan."

Crow sighs and for the first time since I've met him, his façade cracks, just a little. "It's not that I don't like the lad. I've got nothin' against him. But I don't have the time to take him under my charge, Niall. Ye know how tense things are at the moment with the Armenians moving in."

"Aye." Niall shrugs. "I know."

Then he looks to Rory.

I

"Crow's right. He doesn't have the time to take him under his charge. So, you will."

Rory falters for a second, and Crow smirks. "Problem solved."

Niall looks to me and shrugs. "Problem solved."

Sixteen

Ivy

Conor is quiet again on the ride home. He doesn't mention what happened between him and Crow after I left the office, but he doesn't seem to be worried. He's in his own headspace, but his shoulders are relaxed and every now and then he turns to look at me, offering me a small glimpse into his eyes. He's much more at ease than I currently feel. I try to play it cool like he is, but I keep thinking of Archer, desperate for reassurance that it's all going to be okay.

"I imagine ye must be tired," Conor says when we walk in the door. "You can sleep in the bed again. I'll take the sofa."

"Okay." I nod, but I don't want to leave the room, and I can't exactly figure out why. I should be grateful that he's respecting my boundaries. But if I'm being honest, I would be okay with having him sleep next to me. I would be more than okay because I know I'd feel safe. After everything that's happened today, I'm emotionally tapped out, and for once, I just want someone else to do the heavy lifting. I want the guy who put his own life on the line to save mine to sleep next to me and tell me everything's going to be okay. Is that so bad?

It's a terrifying thing to acknowledge. In just the matter of a few simple days, Conor has proved himself honorable in my eyes. I can only hope I don't end up the fool for allowing myself to get caught up in this.

"I want to go visit Archer tomorrow," I blurt.

Conor's eyes move over my face, soft and filled with an understanding that jump starts the heart I was certain had already died. "Sure, we can do that."

We?

I don't argue. I'm not sure how far I can push the boundaries with him yet, and the most important thing is that I see Archer. Relief blooms inside of me as I offer him a small smile. "Thank you. I guess I'll be going to bed then."

He sinks down onto the sofa, kicking off his boots. "Goodnight, wifey."

The word catches me off guard, and I stare at him for a full minute longer than I should. When he looks up at me and our eyes lock, there's a moment between us when everything else ceases to exist. His gaze moves to my lips, and my body shudders when I remember what it was like to kiss him.

I want that again. I want it so much I must be losing my mind. I barely know him. He's mafia. A killer. I couldn't pick a worse guy for me out of a lineup. But I can't deny that the longer I'm around him, the more he draws me into his orbit. It's an impossible want. The moon might as well be chasing the sun.

I can't let Conor know how tormented I'm feeling by this arrangement already. He already did me a favor by saving my life. He owes me nothing else. And at the end of the day, why would he want me?

I swallow down the harshness of my existence in this world

where I don't belong. "Goodnight, Conor."

A shadowed face blocks my exit, and an arctic chill unfurls inside of me. The alley is empty, and I'm more alone than I've ever been. Muerto's piercing laughter echoes off the city walls and the knife in his fist gleams under the moonlight. Tonight, that blade will bite into my flesh and drain the life from me, just like he always threatened.

My heart beats a frantic tempo as I search for a weapon, but there's nothing. Everything I own is gone and there are only two choices. Run, or let him come to me. Desperate to leave him and this nightmare behind, my feet lurch forward before I can think it through, but he tackles me to the ground. His weight is like a concrete block on my chest, suffocating me under his memory. He doesn't speak. He just plunges his blade into my stomach, again and again and again. Blood pools around me and I can feel the light in my eyes slipping away. I think of Archer and how badly I've failed him.

He'll never know how much I loved him.

I wake with a scream, thrashing against the blankets as I try to break free from my nightmare. A shadow passes over me and I scramble away, but his solid grip locks around my arm. The weight of the bed sinks beside me and tears streak down my face as I breathe him in.

"It's okay, Twigs," Conor whispers in the darkness. "I'm right here."

Oxygen fills my lungs, and my racing heart slows when his hand finds my face, soothing me like I never knew I needed.

"It's okay," he whispers again. "It was just a dream."

I'm a mess, and that's the only explanation I have for clinging to Conor's shirt, begging him with a desperation that defies logic. "Please don't go."

I feel silly and weak and vulnerable, but Conor doesn't deny me. Not even for a second. Instead, he pulls back the blankets and helps me back to my spot before he climbs in next to me and drags me against his body, wrapping an arm around my waist to secure me.

His body dwarfs mine in a way that should terrify me, but it doesn't. I know so little about this man, but in his arms, one thing is certain. I trust that he would never hurt me. He would never take something unless it was given freely.

I can't help taking shelter in his strength, burrowing closer to his body. He is warm and muscular and… hard. I realize it when I bump up against his dick with my ass. He must realize it too, because he's gone completely still. He's wearing nothing but his briefs, and I'm in a tank top and underwear. His skin burns into mine, and a swarm of butterflies riots in my belly.

We're breaching unfamiliar territory, and I know if we cross that line, we can't come back from it. But when I squeeze my legs together to smother the want there, it only serves to remind me how empty I am. Because I do want him. I want him in primal ways. His powerful body moving over mine. His rigid flesh inside of me. His mouth on mine while I curl my fingers in his hair. I wonder if he's thinking about it too, but I don't have to wonder for long.

"Christ," he groans. "I don't know if I can do this, Ivy. I want to lay here with ye. I want ye to feel safe. It's just—"

I turn to face him, and before I can talk myself out of it, my fingers find his cheek. I trace the lines of his angular jaw, but my eyes are on his lips. "I want you," I murmur. "And if you want me too—"

Conor's lips are on me then. Demanding and insatiable as he grips the back of my neck, holding me firmly in his grasp as he invades my mouth with an agony I can't deny I feel too. I can't breathe, and I don't want to. I just want to taste him. I want his burning need to consume my flesh, wring me out, and bleed me dry.

His violent craving triggers something even more desperate in me. A reckless abandon I couldn't tame if I threw myself off a cliff. I'm pawing at his body, fingers dragging down his chest while he worships me with his mouth. When I finally palm the huge bulge in his briefs, I shudder with equal parts want and terror. He's so fucking huge, I don't know how he's not going to split me apart. I don't know if I even still work. It's been so long since I was with a man that I chose. Panic steals my breath when it occurs to me that I might be broken beyond repair. Even if I want this more than I've ever wanted anyone else, it might not work. My body might betray me, refusing to accept him. Refusing to get wet for him. But Conor plows through my ridiculous fears when he slides his fingers against my panties and grunts out his satisfaction.

"Christ, ye're soaked for me."

Relief floods my body, followed by a rush of urgency. I need him inside me before my fears overcome this high. "Please," I beg.

He hums his approval as his lips blaze a hot trail over my jaw and down my throat. His hands are warm against my skin, arousing an outbreak of goosebumps all over. I can't remember ever feeling so out of control, so desperate for more. I'm in a drunken haze, completely paralyzed by his eyes as they lay claim to my body.

His fingers are hard, but graceful as he draws the hem of my tank up to my shoulders and exposes the length of my body for his pleasure.

"God, ye have some beautiful tits." He squeezes them in his palms and rubs his face against them.

His tongue lashes against my nipple, and it sends a jolt straight through my core. I arch up into him and reach for a handful of his hair as he does it again. Conor doesn't ask what I like, but he knows. He touches me with just the right amount of pressure, teasing me with his lips and his tongue as he sucks my breast into his mouth.

I'm on the verge of coming from this alone, but then his hand slips down inside of my panties, and it renders me completely defenseless. His fingers dip inside of me, and his breathing intensifies as he drags them back up to my clit, working me over until my body is so strained I plead for him to fracture me.

"Conor…"

"Shhh," he soothes me. "I know what ye need, baby. Just relax."

I can't relax because I'm afraid this feeling is going to disappear, and I'll never have it again. It must be a fluke. A once in a lifetime kind of magic. It's too good to be real.

But it is real, and Conor makes sure I know it when his hot mouth locks around my nipple, torturing me until I splinter apart into a million tiny convulsions. Wave after wave pulses through my body, milking out my release for longer than it's ever gone on before.

I'm breathless and spent, but Conor is just getting started. His fingers glide down and slip inside of me, and he groans at what he's done to me. He likes me this way. Open and raw and vulnerable to him. And it's unnerving, but I don't want it to end. I'm on the verge of telling him how much I want to feel him when he starts to finger fuck me.

"Holy shit." My nails curl into his back, digging into his flesh. He buries his face in my throat, alternating between inhaling me and sucking at my tender skin. He tortures me for so long that I start to entertain thoughts I shouldn't. He must do this sort of thing all the time. It's the only logical explanation for how he could know my body so well.

I don't want to imagine him with anyone else. In this moment, I don't want to believe that anyone else ever existed before me. I've only been with a few men in my life, a serial monogamist to my core. But none of them knew how to please me. Not like Conor. Not like this.

"Oh, God," I cry out.

The tension swells deep inside my core again. It's so intense. I don't think I can hold back, and that's what I'm afraid of. My nails scrape up his neck and into his hair, tugging as I arch into him. The orgasm rips through me with all the force and delicacy of a bullet. I'm sore, breathless, and I feel like I just had an exorcism as I lay there panting, unable to move or speak.

Conor draws in a ragged breath and curses as he slides his palm through the sticky mess between my thighs. I watch with heavy eyes as he palms his dick and coats himself in my arousal. It's the single most erotic thing I've ever witnessed, and I want to watch him do it again and again.

"Fucking hell," he rasps. "I have to warn ye, this is probably going to be quick the first time. I haven't felt a woman's body in a few years."

My eyes move over his face, looking for the lie, but it isn't there. I don't see it. All I can see is his drugged expression as he maneuvers his body between my thighs and grinds his cock against me.

How could that possibly be true? I saw the way the waitress at the diner threw herself at him. I saw women at the club checking him out. He's without a doubt one of the hottest guys I've ever seen, and he's at a strip club practically every night. I still find it difficult to wrap my mind around what he's telling me, but when he starts to push inside me and shudders with every inch, I know it's real.

"Christ, ye're tight." He closes his eyes and releases a shaky breath. "Fuck. Am I hurting you?"

I'm fuller than I've ever been, but I wouldn't let him stop now if he wanted to. "No." I reach up and touch his face. "Give it all to me."

"Goddamn, woman." His hips jerk forward, and he eases himself all the way in, using his forearms to balance his body over mine. "I hope ye know what ye got yourself into. I could fecking live inside ye just like this."

I wrap my arms around his back, and he starts to thrust. His eyes close and his head falls back, and the sounds that rip from his chest are the hottest thing I've ever heard. Like I'm torturing him. Like it's pure torment to be inside of me because it feels so good.

Conor was right that he wouldn't be able to hold back. Every muscle in his body is drawn tight when he curses again. "Fucks sake—"

The words get lost in a long, lamenting growl that vibrates from deep inside his chest. He's balls deep inside of me, dick quivering as he floods my body with hot come. There isn't anything between us. He fucked me raw, and I know when I look up at him, that was his intention.

I also know when he collapses beside me and tells me to give him a few minutes because he has every intention of doing it again... I'm in big trouble.

Seventeen

Conor

I wake to a mess of blonde hair against my chest, and when I glance down, Ivy is still passed out on top of me. She looks peaceful curled against my side, her hand draped over my waist as she uses my bicep for her pillow.

My arm is still wrapped around her too, and it's an odd feeling to have, being so comfortable with her already. I've made a habit of avoiding relationships and even sex since Sammy betrayed me. I've been content to keep myself busy with the brotherhood, and being the new guy, I was never short on shite to do.

Ivy is the first woman I've even wanted to feel wrapped around my dick since I climbed out of the dark hole Brady's death left me in. But lying here with her now, I realize how fecking stupid that is. She isn't here because she wants to be. She's here because she has no other choice. I would do well to remember that before I go and get myself tangled up in her.

Ivy hasn't accepted her fate without a fight. I've seen it in her eyes, the questions in the back of her mind. How long she can survive here until she leaves. There is still a part of her making contingency plans. She hasn't yet figured out how this works, and when she runs, I will give chase. I will track her down and drag her back here, only to have her hate me in the end.

For a few hours, I allowed myself to buy into the fantasy of what Crow said. But this isn't a ready-made family. We aren't two people who met and came together because we wanted this. Our situation is forced, and we can't transform that into something authentic. For Ivy, I will always be another captor.

When she opens her eyes and looks up at me with a sleepy, shy smile, I can't deny that I want to change our fates. She could warm my bed every night, and I could fuck her until my dick gives out. But I need to be realistic. I need to establish boundaries. And I need to do it now.

"Last night was really grand." I roll onto my back and stare up at the ceiling. "I think we both needed that."

Sensing where I'm going with this, she withdraws her hand and untangles herself from my body. I choke down the part of me that wants to tug her back into me.

"It's probably best we don't make a habit of it. I don't want things to get complicated." It's as stupid of an explanation as it sounds like, and Ivy's face falls the moment I say it.

"Right," she mumbles. "It probably wasn't the best idea. I shouldn't have—"

"It's on me," I say gruffly. "You did nothing wrong. I just don't want the lines to get blurred."

She gives me a stiff nod, and I don't know why it feels like I'm digging a deeper hole. I don't need to give her any further explanation, but I want to. Only, the words don't come. So, we lay there in stilted silence, and slowly, she pulls further and further away, and I feel the loss of her all the way down to my dick that's gone soft.

"I guess I should take a shower," I tell her.

"Okay," she agrees, her voice uneven. "No problem."

It would be convincing if we both didn't already know it was a big fucking problem.

I make some coffee and French toast while Ivy is in the shower, and then we eat our breakfast in silence. I stare at my phone, reading through my texts while she gazes out the window. It's awkward, and I really just want to fucking bail and go to the gym or something, but I already told her she could go see Archer. I'm not about to let her make that trek by herself. Not when the Locos are still looking for her.

It reminds me that I still need to discuss that situation with Crow. Otherwise, he might be out of sorts when I tell him I murdered the whole lot of them meself.

"We'll need to head out soon," I tell Ivy. "I have work to do after."

She doesn't look at me. "Okay."

Twenty minutes later, we're in the car and on our way to New Hampshire. Ivy doesn't say a bleeding word the whole way, and I wonder if this is one of those games women play to get you to feel like an arse. But when I glance at her across the seat, I know it isn't.

This sort of despondency is something that's been brewing for a long time. She had her life taken from her. Her freedom ripped away. Now it's happening all over again, and I'm the one who's doing that to her.

Christ.

This was not what I wanted. I shouldn't care how she feels, but I don't want to see her so miserable either. I'm half tempted to tell her to snap out of it, but that's because I'm selfish and I don't want to feel guilty.

Regardless, it makes little difference what I do. The second we pull up to her friend's house and she sees Archer, the smile returns to her face.

Eighteen

Ivy

"Where are we going, mama?" Archer asks from the back seat of the car.

I crane my neck to look back at him. "I'm not sure yet."

Conor loaded us into the car after just a few short minutes at Lacey's. He looked about as comfortable being there as she felt having him in her house. I realize at some point I'll have to explain things to her, but it won't be today.

"Do ye fancy some ice cream?" Conor asks.

"Yes, please!" Archer shouts.

"Ice cream?" I frown. "But it's cold outside."

Conor shrugs. "It's never too cold for ice cream."

Five minutes later, he pulls into a Baskin Robbins and Archer piles out of the car before I can even unbuckle him. He runs straight to Conor, and it makes my heart race just a little too fast when he extends his small hand and reaches out for Conor's larger one.

Conor doesn't hesitate to take it, which surprises me for some reason, though I'm not sure why. He's been nothing but nice to Archer, but I don't want Archer getting attached to him. I can feel it already, and the idea of that terrifies me.

Archer hasn't had a father figure in his life, so I can understand his need for Conor's attention. Under any other circumstances, I would be thrilled that he found someone he feels so comfortable with. But after last night, I'm more certain than ever that I don't plan on sticking around for long, and I don't want Archer's heart getting broken either.

Regardless, I swallow down my nerves as we walk up to the counter and Archer presses his face against the glass to examine the different ice cream flavors.

"What'll it be?" Conor asks.

Archer looks up at him. "What are you getting?"

Conor's lips tilt into an easy smile. "Oreo."

"I'll get that too," Archer offers proudly.

Conor ruffles his hair and turns to me. "How about you, mama?"

My throat is so dry I can barely get the words out. It hits me then, how easy this is. That it could really be like this. We could be a family. Conor could be a part of our lives indefinitely. Except that I can't forget his rejection this morning. He was right that what we did was crazy. Everything he said was true, but it still stung. We shouldn't make this more complicated than it already is, and I don't know why he's being so nice now.

"I'll just have a water," I croak.

Conor shakes his head. "You need to eat. Either you pick out a flavor, or I'll sort one out meself."

Archer giggles. "Why don't you have Oreo too, mama?"

He likes the idea of us together. The three of us unified in our ice cream flavors. And I shouldn't be giving him any more encouragement, but I can't let him down. Not when he's looking at me that way.

89

"Oreo is good."

Conor turns to the cashier. "You heard the lady. Three Oreos in a cup."

Ten minutes later, we've finished our ice cream, and Conor and Archer are playing a game of Tic Tac Toe on a napkin while I watch. As much fun as Archer's having, I'm afraid that Conor will want to leave after this. He's under no obligation to stay, and he's already taken the better part of his day just to drive me up here. But I'm not ready to go yet. Not when I haven't been able to spend any real time with Archer.

When Conor looks up at me, I can't tell if he recognizes that, or it's just my imagination. "What else is there to do in this town?"

Archer contemplates the question for a minute before he decides. "Bowling?"

"Bowling, huh?" Conor scratches his chin. "I suppose we could give that a try. What do you think, mama?"

"Sure." I give Archer a smile and try my best to avoid Conor's gaze. Every second we spend together feels like I'm dodging landmines, and I can't make sense of my feelings.

Conor drives us to the bowling alley, and over the next two hours, he teaches Archer how to play using bumpers and a ramp. I try to make conversation with Archer like we usually do when we're together, but he seems more interested in replicating Conor's every move, and by the time we drop him at Lacey's, I don't feel like we've visited at all.

I'm irritated and frustrated when I say goodbye, but I try to force it down. Archer asks when we're coming back and Conor ruffles his hair and promises soon. I give him a hug and a kiss, and then we get back on the highway. I'm still quiet and tense, a ticking time bomb, and Conor senses it.

"Will ye just tell me what the bleeding hell the problem is already?" he barks.

I glare at him.

"You've been huffin and puffin all day, and I can't figure you out. Did ye not have a good time today? Because Archer and I had a grand time."

"You aren't his father," I snap.

The muscle in Conor's jaw ticks, and I know I've offended him, but I don't care. I'm too far past the point of reason. I'm wounded that Archer wants to spend more time with him than his own mother, and I want Conor to feel the way I do. It's childish and silly, but I'm too emotional to think straight. Between his hot and cold personality and my life being in shambles for so long, logic abandoned me a long time ago.

"I'm your husband." Conor's grip tightens on the steering wheel. "So, in fact, that would make me his step-father. And I wasn't aware you'd get so uptight about me being nice to the kid."

"It's not about the fact that you were nice to him," I bite out. "It's about the fact that he spent all his time with you today, and I barely got to—"

My voice chokes up, and I can't get the rest out. Adding to my embarrassment, real tears have started to fall down my cheeks. Conor pulls the car off onto a gravel side road, driving us into a thicket of trees away from the highway. I feel ridiculous and humiliated, and when Conor reaches out to touch me, it's exactly what I want but everything I don't need.

"It's only because I'm new and exciting," he assures me. "You will always be his number one, Ivy. Ye have no need to worry about that. A boy needs his mother and he always will."

"Stop it," I sniffle. "Quit being nice to me."

He blinks, and then his gaze turns dark. I try to shove him away, but he reaches for my chin and squeezes it between his fingers. "You're my wife. If I want to touch ye, or be nice to ye, or do anything else to ye, I will."

"That isn't what you said this morning."

Conor glares at me, and then his eyes drift to my lips. The car feels too hot, and his fingers are too strong for me to fight, but deep down, I know I don't want to. That's the problem. He's worming his way into every aspect of my life, and I don't like it.

I don't like that my eyes are on his lips too, or that every time I move, I can still feel him inside of me last night. Everything is happening too fast, and the alarm bells are going off, alerting me that this man is dangerous. He's the worst possible threat to me, because I know deep down that I could really fall in love with him. And right now, in such close proximity, I can't think straight. So, I reach for the door handle and yank it open, clamoring out of the car into the fresh air.

"Chrissakes," Conor growls.

He's right behind me, chasing me around the car. I don't know where this dirt road goes, but I intend to follow it. At least until he catches me around the waist from behind and drags me back to the car. I fight him the entire way, elbowing him, cursing him, trying to kick at his shins. My emotional state has taken a nose dive off the deep end.

Conor pins me down against the car with his body weight and grabs a fistful of my hair. "Calm down, ye maniac."

"No," I snarl. But I can't move even an inch with his frame pressed against mine.

"Look at me," he demands.

I don't want to, but a weaker part of me caves in and submits to his request. My eyes meet the blazing green in his, and my heart thumps harder. Louder.

"You belong to me now," he rumbles. "Get that through your thick head before ye try something like that again."

He drives his point home by smashing his lips against mine in a kiss that is both brutal and possessive. At some point, I stop fighting him and melt beneath his touch like a traitor. His hands are all over me then. Clawing at my clothes. Reaching up to cup my breasts and yanking down my jeans. I hear his zipper, and then feel the searing heat of his hard flesh.

When he squeezes himself into me from behind, a feral sound claws its way out of my throat. He's breathing hard, kissing my face and my lips and tugging on my hair while he pounds into my flesh, using me like I'm driving him insane too. I want to believe it. I want it desperately. But I can't give in. I can't allow myself to fall for him.

It doesn't stop me from coming for him though. It doesn't stop me from pleading for him and kissing him back. And it doesn't make me come to my senses and ask him to pull out. When his cock finally unleashes, flooding me with warmth, there's a sick satisfaction in me that proves I'm all sorts of fucked up. Because I needed this from him. I wanted it. And I think the worst part is that Conor knows it.

He kisses me again while his dick softens inside of me, but this time it's sweeter. Deeper. All consuming. He has no reason to kiss me now except that he wants to. And that's what scares me the most.

"I thought you said—"

"I know what I said." He pulls out and tucks himself back into his pants. "Now get your arse in the car and put yourself back together. If we're going to do this, we're not going to phone it in."

Nineteen

Conor

"What are we doing?" Ivy shifts in the passenger seat and stares out the window as I park in front of her friend's house.

I turn off the ignition and twirl the keys around my finger. "Go inside and pack your son's bags. I'll wait here."

"What do you mean?" Her head swivels in my direction, eyes wide.

"He's coming home with us. Tonight."

"Conor, that's not a good idea—"

"It's not up for debate," I tell her. "Your son should be where you are. And I won't have ye moping around the house all day wishing ye could be here instead. It makes no sense."

"This isn't a decision we can make in a few seconds," she argues. "There is a lot more involved with having a kid. We need to decide what's in his best interest and being in a house where—"

"He will never be any safer than he is when he's with me," I say. "And I'm not a bleeding idiot. I know what goes into having a kid.

But I also know that if you don't get your arse in that house to pick him up, then I will. So, what's it going to be?"

Her attention drifts back to the house, equal parts longing and uncertainty in her eyes. I know how much she's missed him. I also know she's scared I'm going to let her down or go back on my word or fuck this up somehow. It would be a wasted breath to tell her otherwise. Ivy needs to figure out on her own that she can trust me, the sooner the better.

"How do you think this is going to go down?" she asks. "Who will take care of him while I'm at work?"

"You will take care of him. Ye're done at the club, I told ye that already."

"Yes, but I'll need another job," she reasons. "Kids cost money and I need to make sure Archer has everything he needs."

"You'll have a card linked to my account by the end of the week," I assure her. "You don't need to worry about money. Whatever he needs, whatever you need, it's yours."

She doesn't answer because she's too busy thinking of all the ways this could go wrong, and I don't have all day. I reach for the door handle, and she turns her wild eyes to me.

"C'mon," I tell her. "We'll do it together."

<hr>

"I think we wore him out today," Ivy says.

My eyes move to the rearview mirror. After all the excitement of coming with us, the kid passed out before we made it ten miles from the house. Ivy is quiet again, but it's a nervous quiet, judging by the incessant fidgeting she's doing beside me. She lasts for all of two minutes before I feel her eyes on me.

"You're good with kids."

I crane my neck to the side, hoping to release some of the tension there. "Like I said, I had some experience."

"Your little brother?"

I jerk my chin.

"What's his name?"

A hot flush crawls up my throat, and I don't want to answer, but it comes out anyway. "Brady."

"Will we meet him too?"

She's treading carefully, aware this conversation is breaching dangerous territory, and yet she's asking anyway. The irrational part of me wants to question her motivations and lash out at her but the logical part of me understands it's innocent.

She told me her story, and I meant it when I said I didn't want to phone this in. When I saw her break down today, it occurred to me how much Ivy needs me. She needs someone to be strong for her when she can't. Someone to do the hard things and take her worries away. And for the first time in my life, I want to be that for someone.

I want to make my wife happy and give her a life she deserves. Not just because it's the right thing to do, but because every time I look at her, I don't want to stop. Right now, the uncertainty of our situation is written in her eyes. But one day, if we make it through this, it might be something else reflected back at me. All of that's going to take time, but we'll never get there if we don't build a foundation of honesty. Maybe it's a mistake on my part, but I decide to give her the same honesty she offered me.

"You can't meet Brady because he's passed on."

"Oh." She bows her head and folds her hands together. "I'm so sorry. I didn't realize."

There's a beat of silence that I'm grateful for until she speaks again.

"Can I ask what happened to him?"

"He got tangled up with the wrong crowd," I answer. "The kid was young, still looking for his place in the world. Thought he could find it with a bunch of piss ass fuckers who like to call themselves gangsters. But things went south, and they killed him."

Ivy swallows hard and I wonder if Brady's story leaves a bitter taste in her mouth, considering her own. "That's really awful."

"Aye, it was."

"I've heard that it helps," she says in a gentle tone. "If you talk about them."

That's the most ridiculous shite I've ever heard. But when I see the genuine curiosity in her eyes, something shifts inside of me, breaking apart the fortress I've kept around Brady's memory these last few years. I can hardly understand what's happening myself when the words start coming out of my mouth.

"He was a good lad. A little shy, a lot goofy. He didn't have a lot of friends. Didn't know how to put himself out there, I guess. But I didn't think it bothered him too much. His nose was always stuck in a book. I couldn't understand it myself, but the kid loved to read. And when he wasn't doing that, he was helping out the neighbors. Not for money, but just because he thought it was the right thing to do. He'd help them with their groceries, trim their lawns, whatever needed doing, he would get after it."

"He sounds like a good kid." Ivy smiles. "How old was he?"

"Only sixteen when he died. I suppose he was at that age where he was trying to figure things out for himself and decided he wanted to prove something. My Pop drilled it into Brady's head he was too soft. It didn't make a difference how much I told him otherwise, there was no getting rid of that notion."

"It sounds like you two were close," she observes.

"Aye, we were. I took care of him. Practically reared the lad meself. We didn't have much in this world, but we had each other. My Pop took his last breath in prison, and Ma made a quick exit with a needle in her arm."

"I'm sorry," she murmurs. "That had to be difficult for you."

I don't answer, but Ivy has the good sense to recognize I've said about all I want to on that subject.

"Is that why you were so sure I was on drugs?" she hedges. "Because of your mom?"

I don't see the point in omitting anything else at this point. It's a sore subject for me, but not for the reasons she thinks. "My ex was a junkie too. It's just not something I have the patience to tolerate anymore. She would have sold her soul for her last fix, and in the end, she did."

There's a quiet understanding between us when she lets that statement rest without pushing it further.

"I'm not close with my family." She lays her head back against the headrest. "They are very conservative. When they found out I was pregnant out of wedlock, they wanted nothing to do with me or Archer."

Without giving it too much thought, I reach over and squeeze her knee. "It's their loss."

A dry laugh wheezes from her throat. "They'd have a coronary if they saw what my life was like now."

"You mean married to the likes of me?"

Her eyes soften when she looks at me. "Just everything. The last couple years have been an epic failure on my part. They would be so ashamed of me."

"It wasn't your fault. You can't control what other people do to you."

Her head dips, and her voice is polluted with the unknown. "Do you think they'll still try to come after me once they know I'm with you?"

"They won't ever come after ye again, Twigs. I'll make sure of it, even if it's the last thing I do."

Twenty

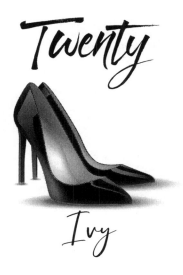

Ivy

Over the next two weeks, our lives fall into a comfortable pattern. Conor gets up long before the day begins and goes to work, leaving Archer and I to eat breakfast alone. After his morning preschool, we spend our afternoons together, playing and reading and treasuring every moment we've been given.

It's everything I ever wanted, and the relief I feel at having him home with me can't be put into words. But I can't deny there's still a part of me that feels empty too. There are still so many uncertainties ahead of us.

From the moment Conor dropped us off at the house, he made it clear that we had rules to live by. We aren't to leave unless he or one of the other guys is around to take us. He said it was to keep us safe, but I also wondered if he was afraid that we were going to leave him.

He hasn't touched me since that day that we picked up Archer in New Hampshire. He left shortly after and has only been home for a few hours each night to sleep on the sofa. He insisted that I sleep in his bed and Archer has his own room set up down the hall. We have everything we need. A roof over our heads, food in our bellies, and we're together again. But Conor's absence is felt every day.

He warned me that his job keeps him busy, but I feel like this is something else. I feel like his absence is intentional, and I don't know what to make of the cold front. I spend far too much time trying to make sense of him. I shouldn't care what he's doing or where he's at, but the thought has crossed my mind that he's at Sláinte entertaining himself with someone else. Perhaps that's why he hasn't touched me.

It doesn't help matters that Archer asks about him several times throughout the day, wondering when he's coming home. I specifically expressed my fears to Conor regarding my son, and a part of me hates him for that. If he never intended to be a presence in Archer's life, then he should have never acted like he was.

Realistically, I know it's not smart to let myself feel this way. Getting upset or trying to figure him out should be the last thing on my mind. What matters is my exit strategy. Since Conor forced me to quit the only job I had, I have no source of income other than what he offers me. He gave me a debit card as promised and insisted that I use it as much as I need.

I never had any intentions of being a kept woman. Regardless of what Conor says, I can't bank on his promises or this marriage working out. So, even though I hate myself for it, I've been withdrawing small amounts of cash every time I go to the store to stash away for an emergency.

But for now, all I can do is sit on the sofa and stuff my face with ice cream until I figure out a better plan. Which is exactly what I'm doing when Conor walks in the door. When our eyes meet, I can tell right away that something isn't right. He looks beat down and exhausted, but even worse is the blood on his shirt. The sight of it compels me to go to him without any further thought. It isn't until I reach him, and my hands are on his body checking him for injury that I realize how silly it is.

Heat rushes up my neck when I look up and catch Conor staring at me.

"Are you okay?" I squeak. "What happened?"

"It's nothing." He cringes when I touch his arm. "Just a flesh wound."

But it isn't a flesh wound I find when I peel back his shirt to reveal the blood-soaked gauze. "Oh my God, Conor! Have you been shot?"

He winces again. "I'm fine. Just lay off of it, will ye?"

My trembling hands fall to my sides and he doesn't miss it. He sighs and takes back the distance between us by tucking a lock of hair behind my ear. "I'm sorry. I've had very little sleep. It's been a long couple of weeks."

"Is it the Locos?" I ask.

Conor shakes his head. "No, I wish it was but it's something else. Another issue we have to deal with."

"You're bleeding." My fingers inch toward the wound again. "Will you at least let me help you get cleaned up?"

His eyes meet mine, and they are too damn pretty for such an ugly world. But it's the reverence I find in the depths of those irises that fires right for my heart. It never really occurred to me until now that he doesn't have anyone to take care of him either. And it hurts to think of him that way. Lonely and alone. He has his mafia brothers and his job, and that's his whole life. But before we came along, this house was just an empty four walls where he came to sleep.

"Where do ye want me?" he asks.

I glance around the room, looking for a spot. "How about the kitchen table? That will probably be easiest."

He walks into the kitchen while I head to the bathroom and dig through the cupboards, hoping for a few first aid supplies. Instead, I'm surprised to find that Conor is stocked with an entire collection, and they aren't the cheap kind. Everything in here is hospital grade. It takes me a few minutes to work my way through it all, gathering what I need before I join him in the kitchen again.

"You have a lot of stuff in there." I toss the supplies on the table.

"Part of the job," he says.

I reach for the first package and pull up a chair beside him, avoiding his watchful gaze while I work. At least, that's the plan. But when I do finally look up, he's grimacing.

"I'm not hurting you, am I?"

"No, it's fine," he says. "It's just the blood. Believe it or not, I still get a bit squeamish around it. Never really cared for it."

"Who does?" I reply.

He shrugs. "Aye, I guess that's true."

We're both quiet for the next few minutes while I clean and re-dress the wound. There's an intimacy to helping a man like Conor when he's in a vulnerable state. I doubt that he allows just anyone to see him this way. He's too stubborn and proud for that.

The wound is in his shoulder, but even a couple inches to the right and this could have ended much differently. He was lucky this time, but what about next time? What if Conor just didn't come home?

It wasn't all that long ago when Muerto would come back to the compound, drunk and bloody from his latest wars on the street. And every time, I found myself thinking that maybe that would be the night. Maybe he would bleed out, and I would finally be free. I hated myself for thinking that way. I hated wishing death on anyone. But when his death meant my freedom, it was the only hope I had to grasp onto.

As I tend to Conor's wound, it occurs to me that the opposite is true. I don't want anything to happen to him. Just the possibility that something could terrifies me, and he recognizes it when I take a deep breath, trying to pull myself together.

"Alright there?"

I apply the last of the tape to his fresh gauze, allowing my fingers to edge just outside the boundary of his skin. "What happens to us if something happens to you?"

He reaches out and toys with a piece of my hair, curling it around his fingers. "That's not going to happen."

My lip trembles and pressure builds behind my eyes, and I feel ridiculous for getting so worked up about this. "But what if it does?"

"Ye're mine now," Conor says with an authority that can't be argued. "No two ways about that, Twigs. When you married me, you married into my family, and my family protects its own. Regardless of whether or not I live to see another day on this earth, no harm will ever come to ye. Crow and my brothers will make dead sure of that."

I force a neutral expression for his benefit, but inside everything hurts. What Conor doesn't understand is that his words don't ease my worries. Because the question I was really asking was what happens to us… *if he's not a part of us anymore.*

To admit that out loud would be to admit that I'm already letting him inside, and I can't do that. He isn't the kind of guy who gives his word lightly. He told me he would protect us, and I believe him. But he never promised to care.

"You haven't been coming home," I say lightly. "Is it because you've been at the club?"

"I've been all over," Conor sighs. "That's my job, Ivy. The lads need me, and I'm there. That's how it works."

My throat is thick with all the things I can't say. "That makes sense."

Conor is quiet again, and I don't know how to navigate these silences with him. He takes control of the situation, reaching out for my hand and weaving our fingers together. "I don't know how to do this," he admits. "I haven't had anyone count on me in a long time."

My gaze moves over our linked fingers, and the weight in my

chest feels lighter, if only a little. "It's okay, we're fine. We have everything we need."

"Things won't always be this way," he assures me. "Rory's got us into some shite right now. The skirt he's been chasing has him wrapped up in her war against mankind, but it'll blow over soon enough."

"Alright."

"Why do I get the feeling ye say that even when everything isn't alright?" Conor asks.

"It is. I have no reason to complain. You've given us a roof over our heads. Food. A safe place for Archer."

"But?" he presses.

Heat blooms in my cheeks as I consider how much to reveal. "I just think maybe we should be honest about expectations from the beginning. I think I have a pretty good grasp on how it works in your world. The wife stays at home, and you guys go out and do whatever, right?"

Conor's lips tilt at the corners. "You mean with whoever, aye?"

I don't get a chance to answer because he reaches out and drags me into his lap before I can give it too much thought. I'm not under any illusions about the size of my frame, but in his arms, I feel even smaller. He feels like a shelter, a safe space, and a disaster in the making. But I can't stop this pull I feel when he's near. And when his fingers graze my arm, it lights a fire inside of my belly I don't know how to put out.

"I meant what I said when I told ye that I haven't been with anyone for years before you." He leans into my throat and breathes me in. "And I've no intention of running off now to stick me dick in everything that has a hole in it. Why would I, when I have you warming my bed at home?"

I relax into him and breathe him in too. It feels reckless to allow myself comfort in his words, but I do.

"I don't know what the Locos got up to," he adds. "But our guys are solid. And when we give our word, we bloody well mean it. We are loyal to each other, and ye best believe we are loyal to our wives. If any one of us got caught cheating on the missus, the others would have our nuts for it if she didn't get to them first. So, don't think that because Muerto did it, I will too. I'm nothing like that piece of shite. Okay?"

"I know you aren't," I admit. "I just... I guess I wanted to hear it from you."

Conor nods against me, and even though he's the one that's wounded, his fingers move over the base of my spine, soothing me in a way that nothing else ever has.

"How's our boy?" he asks. "Settling in okay?"

Our boy.

The words unthaw the coldest corners of my heart, and even if it's wrong to let him say it, I like those pretty words from his lips. I like them so much I want to hear him say them over and over again.

"He's doing good." I turn into him and lean against his chest. "But he's been asking where you are."

"Tomorrow." He tilts his head toward mine and murmurs against my lips. "We should do something with him tomorrow."

"Right." The whisper gets caught somewhere between us, and then swallowed when Conor's lips sink into mine. Already, I'm used to Conor taking what he wants, but this kiss is different. When he kissed me before, it was a means to an end. To claim me. Possess me. Own me. Fuck me. But something has changed between us on a deeper level, and I can't deny it. It's leisurely and passionate. A kiss that could go on forever. I'm breathless and on the edge of sanity when he rolls his hips against my ass, allowing me to feel what I do to him.

"I want you," he grunts. "Say you want me too."

I can't even pretend that I don't. I cave forward, dragging my fingers through his hair and arching my biting hard nipples against his chest. "I want you too."

He groans and nips at my throat as his hand tangles in the mass of my hair. "Say it again. Make me believe it."

I submit to his request, even louder this time. Conor burrows into my collarbone and grazes the sensitive skin with his teeth.

"No, that won't do. I want to hear ye say it when ye're full of my cock."

Twenty-One

Conor

"Conor?" Ivy blinks up at me shyly, and I don't respond. I don't want her to speak right now. I don't want anything other than these few seconds of quiet.

My eyes roam over the naked artistry of the woman sprawled across my bed, sopping up every detail of her curves. She's soft in all the places that I'm not. Inches of milky skin and a hypnotic beauty that I'm quickly becoming addicted to. The subtle bows of her hips taper off into a narrow waist and a valley of silky flesh, rounded out by two plush breasts topped with pink nipples. I have a notion to taste them first, but that wouldn't satiate me. I want all of her. Every intricacy of her body. Every freckle, every scar. There's an urgency inside of me to memorize her wounds and lay claim to her vulnerability.

Muerto owned her, but he never possessed her. With him, she was a bird in a cage, ready to fly away at the first opportunity. It isn't enough to fuck her and tell her she's my wife. I need to make her mine in ways she will never question or doubt. I want her cage door open, but her mind content to stay right here with me.

I peel off my shirt and unbutton my pants, dropping them to the floor. Ivy's chest expands when her eyes move over the bulge in my briefs, and I wonder if she's aware how dark her eyes can be when she's hungry. I palm my dick through the material and toss her a lazy smile. Her body tells the truth her lips refuse. She has nowhere else to be right now, except for in my bed, with my cock balls deep inside her.

My calloused fingers feather over the delicate skin of her ankles, and she shivers when I trace the expanse of velvet all the way up to her knees. She feels like warm honey wrapped in silk, and I hate that any other man has ever touched her. She's mine, and she always has been. I just didn't know it until now.

This cancerous craving breeds deep within, poisoning me from the inside out. I want her words, her thoughts, her smiles and her tears. I want everything from her. It's a fool's errand, but it doesn't stop me from feeding the flames.

All day, she's corrupting my thoughts. I imagine her here, in my bed, laying against my pillow. Her scent burned into my sheets. I have ideas about her riding my cock, kissing me, soothing my aches after a long day. And it only gets worse from there. I think about her proudly wearing my ring, showing the world who she belongs to when she's swollen with my child. These are things I never thought I would want, but fuck if I don't want them with her.

When our eyes clash, I can't bring myself to admit my weakness. The second best thing I can do is bow down between her spread legs and plunge my tongue into her wet pussy. She whimpers, and I sop up her sweetness. Everything else falls away. There's nothing else between us. It's just Ivy, vulnerable to me. Giving herself to me. Riding my face while she grabs handfuls of my hair and comes on my mouth.

"Conor." Her back arches up off the bed, broadcasting her perfect, fuckable tits. I'm starving, manic to taste them when I crawl up her body and latch onto the first nipple in my reach. She hisses, and I pull her flesh deeper, greedy for more while I fumble with my briefs. I fetch my cock and bump against her tight pussy, blundering through the whole performance like it's my first time.

"Chrissakes," I grunt against her. Ivy's lips curve into a smile as she pets my hair with one hand and reaches down to guide me with the other.

I coast into my own little slice of paradise, and it stirs the delirium in my brain. I want to blame it on the pain pills flooding my blood stream, but I know it isn't that. I've missed this. And being inside her now, I can't remember why I ever thought it was a good idea to go without.

"Fuck ye're pretty." My hips crash into hers and she takes it like a champ while her nails dig into my back. "You haven't a clue what you do to men, do ye?"

Her eyes are soft and open as they study my face, seeking out the truth behind my ramblings. I don't want to look away, but she feels so fucking good wrapped around my dick. My eyes are too heavy, and I don't know if I'm falling into a coma or intoxication when my balls draw up and my entire body shudders.

"Fuck." My arms give out, and I collapse on top of her, dick jerking and pulsing as I flood her with what feels like a year's worth of my come.

Her fingers feather through my hair, and I can't move. Don't want to. I stay there, softening inside of her, dragging my lips over hers in an unhurried kiss until we are both too weak to go on.

"Stay with me tonight," she whispers against my neck. "Please?"

I roll onto my side and drape an arm around her waist. "Wouldn't want to be anywhere else, Twigs."

Twenty-Two

Ivy

My heavy eyes blur the room around me as I roll onto my side, straining to listen for the whimper I was certain I'd heard from down the hall. A shadow paints the walls of the bedroom, moving quietly. Conor is already up out of bed, throwing on his briefs.

"It's okay," he assures me. "It's just a nightmare. Go back to sleep."

He doesn't wait around for me to protest, and the last thing I see is his naked back retreating down the hall. My mouth is dry and sticky as I drag myself upright, trying to calm my racing heart. Archer stops crying when Conor's soft voice floods the room, but I won't be sane until I see it for myself. It's a mother's natural instinct to go to him. I need to make sure he's alright.

In a pinch, I throw on Conor's flannel and it hangs all the way down to my knees. Buttoning it haphazardly, I squeak down the hall on my tip toes and lean against the door frame as I peek in on them.

Archer is curled up against Conor's side, his tiny hand securing a place around Conor's bicep. Soft words fill the silence of the dimly lit room while Conor flips through the pages of Archer's favorite book, reading about the adventures of a boisterous puppy.

My heart feels like it's going to explode. Or maybe it already has. This can't be real. My son isn't sitting next to this mobster, soothed by the lulling sound of his voice. Except that he is. Archer watches Conor's face with a reverence that bleeds into the very marrow of my bones. I can see it happening. Archer is falling for him too.

I duck back into the hall and let that sink into my gut. I don't know what I'm doing. This man is not who I would have chosen for Archer to love. He lives a life of violence and chaos and everything that I've been desperately trying to escape. And yet, nobody has ever been so gentle with my son.

Soft, silent tears splash against my cheeks as I slide down the wall and curl my knees inward. I feel like I'm going insane, and the worst part is, I want this. I want this so badly I can taste it. I want Archer to have this strong, enigmatic man in his life. To guide him, protect him, shelter him. But most of all, to love him.

It seems so far from reality, but I can't argue that it's happening right now as I listen to them interact. When Conor reads the last words on the page, I hold my breath, waiting for something to prove me wrong. But instead, all I hear are Conor's hushed words.

"Alright wee one, let's get some sleep, aye?"

The room falls quiet, and for the next ten minutes, I wait for Conor to come out, but he doesn't. When I finally peek around the corner, I wipe my bleary eyes as a smile curves my lips. Conor's large frame is draped over the length of the tiny twin mattress, protectively shielding Archer from the metaphorical monsters under his bed. They are both fast asleep, curled into each other as deep, peaceful breaths fill their lungs.

And it occurs to me right then, I am so fucked.

In the early light of morning, the bed dips when Conor returns to me. A sturdy arm wraps around my waist and pulls me close, tucking me into a body that I could swear was built just to refuge mine. He buries his nose against my neck, breathing me in while he rubs his cock against my ass.

In the back of my mind, the voice of sanity tries to remind me that this isn't normal. This crazy lust-drunk feeling is chemically induced by my traitorous body and I need to be stronger, smarter. But somewhere between last night and this morning, all logic has been sacrificed to the gods of war. Body, heart, and soul—they are at odds with each other, and in the end, I fear that Conor will conquer them all.

"I'll give you one go at what I'm thinking." Conor's calloused palm slips up beneath the sheet to cup my breast, my nipple stabbing at his hot skin.

A secret smile tugs at my lips as I bury my face against the pillow. "What are you thinking?"

"Pancakes." He nips at my shoulder.

A girlish laugh bursts from my chest, surprising me. "I wouldn't have guessed that."

"No?" His other hand slips between my thighs, fingers gliding through the stickiness that's already gathered there.

I arch against him, splaying my legs wide open like a lovesick fool. "Definitely wouldn't have guessed that."

Conor rolls me onto my back and mounts me, lowering his body between my thighs and yanking down his briefs like a caveman. "Maybe with syrup. Or strawberries. I haven't decided yet."

I wrap my legs around his waist when he pushes inside of me, and his eyelids grow heavy with drunken satisfaction. Conor doesn't just like to fuck me, he likes to own me. He's been rough with me. Possessive, hard, demanding. But right now, he's soft and slow, rolling his hips in and out of me like he has all day to stay just like this.

He kisses me and inhales me and whispers in my ear how much he likes being inside of me. I come twice for him, and then he finishes with a tormented groan that seems to go on forever. When he collapses into the bed and drags me back against his chest, I'm still trying to figure out what just happened. I can't be sure, but it feels like my husband just made love to me.

"Just a few more minutes," he murmurs sleepily. "Then pancakes."

Twenty-Three

Conor

The phone in my pocket chimes again, and I ignore it, turning my attention back to Archer. His eyes are wide with an innocence only a child can possess as he watches the prairie dogs poke their heads up at Franklin Park zoo.

"Everything okay?" Ivy asks.

I secure an arm around her waist and pull her against me, secretly groping her ass while my lips violate the soft skin around her ear. "It's grand."

Her eyes fall shut, and she leans into me, but it's a false comfort. Every time she gives in, her mind resists, and little by little the tension bleeds back into her body. She's still fighting this connection between us. Her mind is a puzzle, and at times, I don't know if it's me or her own feelings she's at war with.

She looks up at me with eyes that betray her confliction. "If you have stuff to do, you don't have to stay."

My jaw scratches against her cold skin, and she shivers. "Aye, I have stuff to do. Like spending the day with you and Archer."

She buries her head in my chest to hide her expression, but I want to believe that for right now, she's content. Just as Archer is over the next three hours while we follow him over every reasonable inch of the zoo. He presses his face against each glass enclosure we come across, carefully examining the little critters that peek back out at him. He chatters excitedly, and I catch a few rare glimpses of Ivy's pretty smile. And I think she should be smiling like that all the time. She should also be wearing my ring on her finger, but it's something I've yet to sort out.

"Thank you," she tells me on the drive home. "That meant a lot to him. He had so much fun today."

I glance over at her. "They're only wee for a little while. They should enjoy every second of it."

She melts into her seat and sighs. "I'm exhausted."

I reach over and squeeze her knee. "Then ye better get a cup of coffee when we get home. The night is still young."

She blinks. "What do you mean?"

"I had a notion I might take ye out this evening."

The gears in her mind are turning, that much is obvious, but I don't know what's going on in there until she speaks. "What about Archer?"

"I've already sorted out a sitter. Rory is game to hang with the little lad."

"Really?" She arches a brow.

"Aye, he loves kids. Can't wait to have twenty or so of his own."

Ivy's fingers tangle together in her lap as she stares off into the distance. She's nervous. It's natural that she should be, and that's what makes her a good mother. But at some point, she'll need to learn to trust me.

"The lad will be just fine," I promise. "We look after our own. No harm will ever come to Archer while he's with Rory. I wouldn't ask him if I didn't trust him with my own life."

She digests my words in her own time, and I don't bother her until she's settled into the idea. "Alright." She shrugs. "I guess a couple hours out would be okay."

"What are we doing here?" Ivy eyeballs the back door of Sláinte like it's the gate to hell.

Ignoring her tone, I reach down to help her out of the car. "Thought we'd pop in to say hi to the lads."

She takes my hand, but her back is rigid. I didn't think she'd turn up her nose at the club, but I suppose this is the part of the date where everything goes to shite. We've already been to dinner—a nice Russian restaurant owned by a mate in the Back Bay. Ivy kept insisting she didn't need anything fancy, and I almost laughed when her eyes roamed over the menu prices. That sort of thing is nothing to me, but it's a lot to her. Sometimes, I'd like to forget that she was sleeping on the streets and going without food just a short time ago. Those days are over, and I want her to know it.

"Are you sure this is a good idea?" She slips her hand into the elbow I offer as we walk toward the back door.

"I think it's a grand idea. This is where all of my mates are, and I want ye to get to know them."

She looks nervous as all get out but doesn't argue about it any further.

"There's just one wee little detail." I stop before we go inside and turn to face her. "It's an important one."

Her brows pinch together in concern. "What is it?"

"The lads don't know we're married. Not just yet. We need to keep it that way for a while."

She stares down at her shoes like they hold all the answers to her problems. "I won't say anything."

If she has any questions about my reasoning, she doesn't say so. It's a discussion I intend to save for later, when I have more time to explain the dynamics of our brotherhood and Crow's request. For now, I lean down and kiss her just because I can. Once her lipstick is good and thoroughly messed up, I'm satisfied that the lads won't have any question about who she belongs to anyway.

Inside, the club is packed like it usually is on Friday nights, and the lads are scattered throughout the bar. I spot Crow and Mack through the crowd and make a beeline in that direction with the intention of introducing Ivy to her. But before we get that far, Reaper appears out of nowhere.

"Conor, I need a quick word with ye in private," he says.

He wants to talk shop and being that I asked for his help keeping eyes on the Locos, this could be important. I don't want to abandon Ivy to the wolves, but I know Crow's missus will take good care of her.

I give her arse a good squeeze and bring my lips to her ear. "Head on over to Crow. I'll be back shortly."

She looks less than pleased when I send her on her way, and I tell Reaper we need to be quick. We sneak into Crow's office for a bit of privacy and I get straight to business.

"What have ye heard?"

"You were right," he says. "They've been looking for her. I snatched up one of their latest recruits, not a very bright one at that. Only had to cut off three of his fingers to get him talking."

Ronan discusses the gory details of his job with a blank face. He's got the stomach for torture, but right now the specifics don't matter. I need to know what was said, and I tell him so.

"The lad says the Locos want to perform some sort of honor killing," Ronan goes on. "They all plan to have a go at her first. Then—"

"Okay." I bite back the bile that rises in my throat. "I get it."

He shrugs. "Crow gave us the go ahead to start finishing them off. I've got two fresh ones in the basement now if ye want to have a wee bit of fun with them."

"Can it wait until tomorrow morning?"

"Aye." He nods.

"Grand. I'll be back then."

"Ye best keep a close eye on her," Ronan adds. "You know this is going to start a war."

There isn't even a question in my mind when I answer. "Then it's a war they will have."

Twenty-Four

Ivy

I never made it across the bar to Crow and his wife. The minute Conor disappeared into the crowd, I found an empty table and sat down, thinking it was the safer option. Crow doesn't seem to care for me too much, and I had no interest in pretending otherwise while I waited for Conor's return.

I don't know why he brought me here, but my gut tells me there's going to be an issue, and after only a couple minutes, there is.

"Hey."

I swivel around to find myself caught in the sights of a burly patron palming a glass of whiskey with his meaty hand.

"Hi," I answer out of politeness.

"I've been wondering where you were." His eyes rake over my body with a familiarity that sickens me. "Haven't seen you around the last few weeks."

I swallow down the hot humiliation threatening to choke my voice. "What do you mean?"

| |

"I haven't seen you up on stage," he clarifies.

I offer him a weak smile. This is exactly what I was afraid of. One night of dancing, and already, it's starting. Everyone in this club will think they can have a go at me simply because I worked here and showed them my body.

"I don't dance anymore," I inform him.

The guy smiles but it isn't at all friendly. "That ain't how it works. When Crow hires a dancer, you're done when he says you're done. You must think I'm pretty stupid."

"Not at all." My hands squeeze into fists at my side, and I hate Conor for putting me in this position. "I'm just informing you that regardless of what you might believe, I no longer dance here."

He cocks his head to the side, studying me. "Do you think you're too good for me, is that it?"

"Will you please just go away," I snap. "There are plenty of other women—"

"Look here." He snatches my arm and drags me up out of my seat. "You lose the lip and give me a lap dance, and we'll forget about your shitty attitude."

"Leave me alone, asshole." I try to shove him away, but the guy is like a brick wall, and I swear it only makes him more excited. He hauls me even closer and grabs a handful of my ass like he has that right.

"If you're nice, maybe I'll let you suck my dick too."

My lips purse together with the intention of spitting in his face, but before I get the opportunity, he's dragged backward and dropped to the floor with a single punch to the head. Conor is between us, his fist still clenched at his side while his eyes move between us in question. They aren't the calm, soothing green I've come to know. Right now, they are a raging sea of pure wrath, and my immediate instinct is to step back.

The instigator scrambles to his feet, dazed, and Conor grabs him by the shirt. "What the feck do ye think you're doing?"

"Lay off." The guy pushes against him. "She's a fucking dancer. I was just—"

"You were just touching what's mine, and now ye can say your final words before I bury what's left of your body in the Charles River."

"Do we have a problem here?" Crow interjects, his eyes darting between the three of us.

"Fecking right we do," Conor bites out. "This chump thought he could touch my…"

The words get caught in his throat as he looks to Crow. He stopped himself before he could call me his wife, but right now, that's all I want him to do. I wrap my arms around my chest and wish to God he'd never brought me here tonight.

Crow inserts himself between Conor and the other guy. "Is that true? Did ye cop a feel of this girl?"

"She's a dancer! What the fuck does it matter. That's the whole point, isn't it?"

"She's not a dancer anymore," Crow answers. "And even if she were, I believe ye're well aware of the fact that's not how we do things around here, Slick."

His face pales, and Crow gestures to Conor. "Take him downstairs and teach him a lesson he won't soon forget. Just make sure he's breathing when he leaves here. Ivy, you can come to the office to visit with Mack."

I don't want to go, but Conor won't even look at me. He's hell bent on retribution and so deep in his anger that he's already dragging the guy toward the basement.

"Come on." Crow gestures for me. "He'll be back soon enough."

"So..." Mack says.

I nod in answer. We've been sitting in silence for the last five minutes and it's beyond awkward. I'm not exactly in the frame of mind to visit with anyone right now but it occurs to me that I should probably make the effort.

"Thank you for the clothes," I tell her. "Conor mentioned you picked them out."

"Of course. It's probably the only time I'll ever get to shop in those teeny tiny sizes. It was fun while it lasted."

My eyes move over her, and it doesn't take long to understand what Crow sees in her. She's absolutely gorgeous. Dark hair and a pretty face are just a couple of her best features, but I can't find a single thing that she shouldn't be proud of. She's lean and strong in a way that can only be earned in a gym, and I admire her for that.

"You look amazing," I assure her. "I wish I was in such great shape."

She shrugs and pats her belly. "I have a weakness for Dunkies, and I pay for it. But it's totally worth it."

The room falls quiet again, and I start getting sucked back into my own thoughts before Mack interrupts me.

"Okay, I just have to say it," she blurts. "I think it is so freaking cute how wrapped up in you Conor is. I've never seen him like this."

"Oh?" I squeak. "Really?"

She nods enthusiastically and scoots closer to me on the couch, waving her hands about as she talks. "He's such a grumpasaurus sometimes, but you can't help loving the guy. I'm so happy he's finally found someone to make him act like a total caveman."

"I wouldn't say that." I wrap my arms around myself. "He's not really with me by choice."

"Oh, please." Mack laughs. "Crow told me about your situation. Conor wouldn't have married you if he didn't have major feels for you."

She seems so certain of it that I don't want to argue, but I don't know what to believe anymore.

Mack pats my arm. "Honey, he wouldn't be down in that basement fucking up that guy for touching you if he didn't care. It might seem barbaric, but that's his way of saying he cares about you. He'll protect you. And he damn sure won't let anyone degrade you."

I release a breath and laugh. "It really is a different world, huh?"

"I know it's a lot," she says. "Living this life is kinda nuts, believe me when I say I get that. When I first got into it, I thought I hated every one of these mafia guys. But it takes a while to see that they are the best brothers you could ever ask for. And things with you and Conor will get easier too."

"I hope so."

"You'll have to come hang with me and the girls one of these days. Trust me when I say that we love our husbands, but it doesn't mean they don't drive us batshit crazy half the time either."

"That would be nice," I tell her, and I mean it.

"Good." Mack gives me a conspiratorial wink. "Now that we've settled that, we can move onto the important stuff."

"Like what?" I ask.

She walks over to Crow's desk and wiggles a Dunkies box with a devious smile. "Like what kind of donuts are your favorite?"

Twenty-Five

Conor

"Have enough yet, mate?"

Slick sputters out a choked affirmative, but it doesn't make a bit of difference. He caved within the first five minutes of seeing Reaper's room of torture. He started carrying on like the spineless coward he is when it came down to it.

The racket only got worse when I broke his arm. That should have been it. Crow gave me orders, but I can't let it die that easily. I have an example to set. To him or any other maggot who thinks they can touch what's mine.

There is no satisfaction in the cracking of his bones as I count off the fingers on his left hand one by one. It irks me that I can't even tell him what the real crime is. Crow has me bound to silence about Ivy's position in my life and this club, and it rubs me the wrong way. He sure as shite wouldn't be willing to do the same if it was Mack. From the minute he claimed her, he made no bones about it to everyone who might think of toying with her.

Regardless, Ivy is alive, and that's better than the alternative. I should be grateful, but the uncertainty of our future pricks me like a hot knife. She can't even follow a simple request from me, which is rule number one of being a mafia wife. I don't know how in the bleeding hell I'm going to keep our marriage a secret when I want to murder every tosser who looks her way.

I need to blow off some steam, so I beat the hell out of Slick with my bare hands. I fuck up his face and hit him in the kidneys until he'll be pissing blood for a good week, and that's when Ronan decides to interrupt me.

"What?" I scowl at him.

He offers Slick a cursory glance. "I think the bloke has had enough. He won't be bothering with your missus anymore."

"Would ye have the same sympathy for him if it were your wife?"

Ronan's brows pinch together because I just fucked up, and he's too smart to miss it. I may as well have printed him an invitation to the wedding with that statement. The gears in his head are turning, and he's already figured it out, but he won't say anything. Ronan understands better than anyone the madness a woman can impart on a man.

"Get back upstairs to Ivy," he suggests. "Go home and cool your jets."

I glance at the sorry sack of shite curled up on the floor, his face a bloody mess and his hand so swollen he won't be able to use it for a good month if he's lucky. Satisfied that he'll think of me every time he tries to spoon feed himself, I leave the room and head back upstairs to collect Ivy. Crow is at his desk in the office, fiddling with his phone while Mack and Ivy talk quietly on the couch.

"Get everything sorted?" Crow glances up at me.

I nod. "I'm taking Ivy home."

"Aye, I think that's a good idea."

The return trip is quiet, and Ivy stares at me throughout, but I can't look at her right now. I don't want to unleash on her when I'm in a prick of a mood, but she needs to understand that when I ask her to do something, it just has to be that way.

When we get to the house and relieve Rory of his babysitting duties, he notices something isn't right, but he isn't the type to bother me about it. After giving us a quick report of the night, he makes himself scarce and disappears out the front door.

Ivy's still in the parlor, standing there with her arms hanging awkwardly at her sides. I steal a quick glance at her and shake my head. "Are you okay?"

"I'm fine," she answers flatly.

"Grand. Then you should get yourself cleaned up and get some sleep."

She glares at me. "Is this because he touched me?"

I don't want to have this conversation right now, and I let her know as much. "I have shite to do. I'll be back after."

"Just tell me." She crosses her arms in the way that women do when they're pissed. "Do you think I led him on or something?"

"Of course I don't fecking think that," I snap.

"Then why are you pissy with me?"

"Because ye can't even follow a simple goddamn request." I scrub a hand over my face. "If you had just done what I'd asked, everything would have been fine."

"You can't seriously believe that." The vein in her neck pulses with repressed anger. "You brought me on a date to the same place I took my clothes off for the world to see. What were you thinking?"

"I was thinking that's where I like to spend my free time and you could come along too."

She mocks me with a caustic laugh. "Did it ever occur to you that maybe I didn't want to? That from the beginning, I haven't had a say in any of this and I'm just along for the ride?"

If her intention was to wound me with those words, she's done a bang-up job of it. This conversation is going nowhere fast, but I can't let it die.

"I saved your arse when I could have just put a bullet in your head. Have you even thought about that? I gave ye a home. A safe place for Archer. I don't know what more ye fecking want from me. Ye're alive, and ye haven't been captured by the Locos, so it seems to me ye have it pretty good."

Her head dips, and all the fight leaches from her body. "You're right. That should be enough."

But what's she's saying is that it isn't. And it only confirms what I've been thinking myself all along. She's here because she has to be. She'll never see me as anything else than the man who fucked up her life. I don't know what the bleeding hell I've been doing, playing house with her like we're a fucking family. Kissing her and fucking her and whispering bullshit words in her ear at night. If it wasn't clear before, it's perfectly clear now. Ivy despises me for what I did, and she always will.

I'm no hero.

And I guess it's time I remembered that.

Twenty-Six

Conor

"Are you alright, mate?" Reaper's voice breaks through the stillness of the basement, and I blink up at him.

His eyes are on my hands, still speckled with the blood of the two useless wastes of human life I extinguished tonight. It didn't occur to me to wash it off, and it speaks volumes to how far I've come since I first began. But the fact that Reaper is even sitting here at all, asking me if I'm okay speaks volumes about him too.

The man was practically a robot when I met him, but his wife Sasha humanized him in ways I never thought possible. When I see them together, there is no denying the pure love in his eyes. They would die for each other. They will fight for each other. It's the kind of love that starts wars, and I've always been a little envious of that.

We might be a crazy, murderous foul lot of muppets, but at the end of the day, we want to come home to a warm bed and a beautiful woman who loves us in spite of all that. I never fancied myself a bloke to want such things, but in my drunken state, I can admit that I do. But after what Ivy told me tonight, I don't know that I'll ever have it.

"She isn't just a girlfriend," I slur. "It's a lot more complicated than that."

Ronan acknowledges my drunken confession in his usual fashion. "If that wasn't bleeding obvious, I don't know what is."

I take another swig of the half empty whiskey bottle in my hand. "She isn't like your missus."

"How do ye mean?" Ronan asks.

"She isn't with me because she's crazy about my dumb arse. She only married me because she had no choice."

Ronan shrugs and snatches the bottle out of my hand. "They don't have to like you in the beginning. Time will sort out her feelings."

"Maybe." But I have other ideas. An idea that only a drunk bloke would think was a good one. "Would ye mind giving me a lift home?"

The house is quiet, and after a little investigation, I find Ivy asleep in Archer's bed. I expected as much, but it doesn't make it feel any less like a slap in the face. She wants nothing to do with me, and if her words didn't let me know it earlier, this definitely does. Still, I hesitate in the doorway, watching her sleep while I consider my intentions.

There's no coming back from what I'm about to do. The truth will change things. It will open my eyes and probably fuck everything up, but I'm done playing make believe with her. I need to know how she really feels, and there's only one way to do that. But it doesn't make me any less apt to go to her. To get down on my knees and beg her for sweet words and false promises. Promises that she could feel something else for me like the way I feel for her right now.

Only, that would make me weak and I can't ever be weak. Not with Ivy. There's one solution to this clusterfuck, and it isn't in this room. I pull the door shut, obscuring her from my view before I stumble down the hall to our room. My eyes dart over the space that smells like her. Warm and inviting and so sweet I can almost taste her.

Her things are mixed in with mine. Her clothes in the dresser, shoes in the closet. She has so little, but what she does have is here. I rifle through all of it before I find what I'm looking for, tucked away in a small compartment of her backpack. The tattered pages of her journal that hold the secrets I've often seen her scrawling when she doesn't think I'm paying attention.

I flip through the first few pages, dated a year ago, and what I find turns the whiskey in my gut sour. It's a detailed account of her life with Muerto. A no holds barred narrative of the sick things he would do to her and the threats he used to keep her compliant. There are so many specifics I can't stomach to read through them all.

In the later entries, her writing changes. Hurried notes scrawled in haste about how much she misses her son. On other pages, there might only be one sentence, but that sentence says it all. She prays for death to come, the only thing she believes will set her free.

I retrieve the flask from my jacket and crack it open. It's the only way I can see fit to get me through the rest. But there are so many pages of this shite. Too fucking many. Maybe it's selfish, or maybe I'm weak, but I can't finish them. A sinking feeling weighs me down as I flop onto the bed and skip ahead to the part where she meets me. Before I even get started, I know I'm not going to like what I find.

Our situation is different, but in many ways it's the same. Ivy was right that it doesn't matter what I do or say. In the end, what it boils down to is that she's here because she has no other choice. These same thoughts are reflected back at me in the pages of her journal.

I don't know how I got myself into this mess, but I need to find a way out. I can't be with a guy like Conor. I can't be stuck with him for the rest of my life. I just need to get through this. I need to get as far away from him as I can. I hate him. I hate him so much it pains me to pretend otherwise for even a second.

I slam the pages of the notebook shut, tucking it away from my sight. If I had any notions that this would end differently, I'm over that now. The truth is right there in black and white. Ivy hates me and that's all I need to know.

Twenty-Seven

Ivy

"When is Conor going to be home, mama?" Archer asks.

"I'm not sure, buddy."

It's been almost a week since our argument, and I've barely seen him at all. He leaves before we get up in the morning and comes home long after we've gone to bed every night.

"But we made him dinner," Archer whines. "Do you think he'll like it?"

"He will," I assure him, even though I texted Conor over an hour ago and still haven't received a reply.

I can't bring myself to admit that I've lost all hope. Not when Archer is so desperate to see him. But when the front door opens and Conor appears, the ache in my gut mellows, if only a little.

"You're here!" Archer squeals as he runs across the room and flings himself into Conor's arms.

"Hey, squirt." Conor ruffles his hair and offers him a smile, which is more than I've seen from him lately.

"We made you dinner," Archer says proudly.

"Aye, that's what I hear." Conor rubs his belly. "Good thing too because I'm starving."

Archer leads him to the table, and I remain rooted to the floor in the kitchen. Conor barely glances at me before he takes a seat, and the chill penetrates my skin from here. He hasn't touched me. He hasn't kissed me. He hasn't said more than two words to me over the course of the week. And I don't want to admit that this cavernous space cracking open inside my chest might be what I think it is.

Heartbreak.

I miss him. I miss him terribly, and I want to make things right, but I don't know how. I don't know if I'm capable of hurting Conor, but I know that he hurt me. His shame and reluctance to tell his friends that I'm his wife cuts me to the core, and he owes me an explanation for that. There are so many things I want to say, but the words won't come. In the end, we are both too proud or stubborn to admit defeat. So instead, we sit down at the table together and eat our feelings.

"Do you like it?" Archer asks.

"Aye, it's very good," Conor says. "Thank you, little fella."

"Mom did most of the work," Archer supplies. "She's a good cook."

Conor meets my eyes, and for a split second, I want to believe it's regret I see there before they turn to stone all over again. "Aye, she is."

He concentrates on shoveling his dinner into his mouth, so he can get out of here. I know it before he says so, and I'm proven right when he pushes back his chair.

"Thanks for dinner. I have to get back to work."

"Whyyyyy?" Archer pouts.

"Can we talk?" I blurt.

Conor checks his phone, still avoiding eye contact. "A quick one."

I tell Archer to go play in his room for a couple minutes, and he reluctantly stomps down the hall. I wait until his door is shut before speaking. "Is there something going on?"

"Like what?" Conor taps out a message on his phone.

"You haven't been home. You've barely spoken to me. I just—"

"Welcome to being a mafia wife." His tone is so flat, I can't stand it.

I hate that I'm getting emotional, or letting it get to me at all. I'm shaking, my hands itching to rip that phone out of his hands and throw it into the garbage. "I get that you're still pissed at me, but we can't make this work if—"

His eyes snap up to mine, and they are brimming with a darkness I haven't seen in him before. "That's exactly what we're fecking doing here, Ivy. We're making the best of a shitty situation. The only way to make this work is by ignoring the fact that we're chained to one another for life."

I feel my body crumpling in on itself. My stomach is full of lava, eyes burning with unshed tears. What a fool I've been to think that Conor could love me. Maybe for a second, it was possible. But now it's painfully obvious he's miserable, and he'd rather be anywhere else than here.

"Chrissakes." He turns his back on me when he sees the vulnerability in my face. "I don't know what else ye want from me."

"Nothing." My voice wavers. "I don't want anything else from you."

"Did you get everything out of your drawers?" I ask Archer.

He nods and clings to the teddy bear Conor bought him at the zoo. "Where are we going?"

I arrange a pile of our bags outside the front door. "On an adventure."

Archer doesn't look convinced, and I don't blame him. I hate everything about this situation, but if there's one thing I know for certain, it's that I can't wait for things to get any worse. The only way to preserve both of our hearts is to get out now, while we still can.

It doesn't matter if I only have a thousand dollars and the clothes that Conor bought us. We will figure it out. We will get on a bus and go far, far away, and we will stay in a shelter if we have to. As long as we're safe and we're together, that's all that matters.

But even I'm still not convinced when I glance at Archer and see the questions in his eyes. He's attached to Conor, and he's not the only one. The idea of leaving this house behind feels like we're leaving the only real home we've ever had. We'll never see Conor walking through this door again. I'll never feel his body curled against me in the middle of the night. And Archer will probably never stop blaming me for taking him away from the only man he's ever loved.

I feel like a horrible mother for allowing it to happen in the first place. I believed Conor. I thought he wanted us. But his actions and his words have proved my worst fears to be true. Now, we're all out of options and Archer and I have to move on.

"Leave the door cracked," I choke out. "Wait here while I talk to the driver."

I walk down to the sidewalk where the cab is waiting, ten minutes earlier than expected. The driver is engrossed in his phone when I open the back door and speak through the plate glass divider.

"You're here for Misty?" I ask, giving him the fake name I provided when I ordered the cab.

"Yeah, that's me," he mumbles.

I ask him if he can open the trunk while I meet Archer at the top of the stairs, grabbing our bags along with his hand. By the time we get back down to the sidewalk, the driver is out of the car.

"Let me give you a hand with that," he says.

I hesitate when he reaches for the bags. Maybe it's just my paranoia, but something feels off. He's wearing a baseball cap pulled low over his eyes, and his arm is in a sling. He couldn't possibly work for the Locos, or at least that's what I want to believe. But suddenly everything about this situation feels wrong, and it isn't until I get a whiff of his cologne that I realize why.

Slick was wearing that same cologne. I couldn't forget it if I tried. And even though I can't see his eyes, I know in my gut it's him. It can't be a coincidence that he's here now.

I try to stay calm as I let go of Archer's hand. We've rehearsed this a thousand times. I just need to get him back in the house. That's all that matters right now. "Archer, did you forget Mr. Potato Head?"

His eyes widen when he looks up at me, acknowledging our secret code, and then they slowly move to the guy.

"Go back in the house and grab him," I instruct. "Better make it quick."

Archer doesn't let me down. He follows the protocol we have in place. The same one I've made him practice again and again. He darts back up the stairs and shuts the door behind him, and when the lock clicks into place, I spring into action.

I pull a wad of cash from my pocket and try to hand it to Slick. "You know what, we're going to be a while. I think I'll call a cab later once I'm sure we've got everything."

He reaches out for the cash but grabs me by the wrist instead. "Do you think I'm stupid?" He yanks me against him, and that's when I feel the end of a gun against my rib cage. "Get in the fucking car, and do it without making a scene, or I'll make sure your son comes along for the ride too."

I swallow every instinct that screams at me to revolt and run. Something in his eyes tells me I won't make it a block down the street before he shoots me, and then Archer too.

"Please don't do this," I whisper.

He cocks the gun, and my breath dies in my chest. "Too late, bitch. Now get in the fucking car."

Twenty-Eight

Conor

"**C**onor," Crow barks at me. "Get the feck out of here."

I look up from the sofa in his office, scrubbing the sleep out of my eyes.

"Ye're completely worthless to me right now." He tosses my jacket at me. "What the bleeding hell is going on with you?"

"He's got lady problems," Reaper chimes in.

Crow huffs. "Ye told me this wasn't going to be an issue. And yet here you are, moping around all week like someone stole your lollies."

I sit up and crack my neck from side to side, trying to release the tension that's accumulated since I took up napping on Crow's sofa. "There isn't an issue."

He curses under his breath and Ronan butts in again. "He thinks his missus hates him. That's why he's all bent out of shape."

"I never said that." I glare.

"Aye, you did," Reaper insists. "When ye were whining last night after ye got your mitts on the whiskey."

Crow snickers. "That's it? That's the fecking problem? Ye're all bent out of shape because Ivy hates you?"

"It's not funny," I counter.

He looks to Ronan. "Aye, it is. Do you recall how much my missus hated me when she came blasting into this place? That's the nature of the beast. You better develop some thicker skin if ye can't handle a little fire in the pan."

I get what Crow's trying to say, but our situations are different. It might have worked out for him, but he wasn't exactly holding Mack hostage either.

"Besides—" Crow walks over to his desk and pours himself a drink. "That girl doesn't hate you. I've seen the way she looks at you. Ye're just being a mophead."

That much is probably true. The way I left things tonight wasn't my finest moment. Ivy went out of her way to make an effort, and I threw it back in her face because my pride was wounded.

"Get your arse home and make it right," Crow says. "Then get your head on straight. I need ye to pull it together."

"Aye, I will."

The house is dark when I get home, and I don't need to flip on the lights to know something isn't right. It's too early for Ivy to be in bed. Even if she was, she always leaves the lamp on for me. But when I walk down the hall, my gut twists with what I already know I'll find.

All of her things are gone. And Archer's too. The house is empty, and it takes a full minute for that to sink in.

She left me. Just up and left without so much as note. Can't say that I blame her after the way things have been. Crow was right. I am a dumbarse, and now my girl is gone and the wee lad too, and I'm sitting here alone wondering where they might be. But then I wonder if it even matters.

If she's out of the city, and she's safe, maybe that's for the best. Maybe that's exactly what she needed. I know it's what she wanted.

But it isn't what I want. I can't get my head around that. The idea that I won't ever kiss her again. Or hold her again. I'll be coming home to an empty bed every night where she should have been.

Fuck.

I let her down. I let them both down.

I told her in the beginning that I'd come after her. And I know now that I meant it. Because if nothing else, I need to know she's safe. I need her to look me in the eyes and tell me that it's over. Even then, I probably won't let them go. Because I need them. I love them, and she can hate me for as long as she wants because I'll do whatever it takes to get her back.

I comb through her empty drawers, looking for any evidence she might have left behind. But everything is gone. She just deleted her-self from my life. Her clothes, her shoes, her scent. None of it's here, and it isn't right.

The only thing I find is the last thing I'm expecting. Her journal is still tucked beneath her pillow on her side of the bed, forgotten. And I can't forget how badly things imploded the last time I looked at this, but it doesn't matter now. My feelings don't matter. I need to make sure she's safe.

I crack the pages and flip through to the end, and that's when I notice the gap. The pages I read before weren't the last pages she wrote. Not by a long shot. She started again in a different section of the journal, and when I see the words written there, I collapse back onto the bed.

I miss him. I miss him so much it hurts. But I know that I can't make him love me. I just wish I'd never fallen for him.

My heart drums out a war cry in my chest. *She fell for me. She wants me.* It's right here in black and white, but now she's gone.

From somewhere in the house, something creaks, and I shoot up from the bed, whipping out my Glock. I listen for the noise again as I slink down the hall, but it's quiet. Archer's room is open, and everything is just as Ivy left it. The bed is made, but all his toys are gone. It stabs at me all over again.

And then I hear a sniffle. A tiny inhale of air, and my pulse pounds. Someone is under the bed. Ivy and Archer are gone, but someone is under the bed. I kneel down, ready to kill whoever the fuck thought they could come into my house. Only, what I find there is a pair of terrified, tear-soaked eyes.

"Archer?"

He splutters, and a sob bursts from his chest when he realizes it's me. I reach in and drag his tiny body toward me, wrapping him up in the safety of my arms.

"It's okay, buddy," I whisper. "It's okay. I'm here. I'm not going to let anything happen to you."

He clings to me, squeezing me so tight it scares me. Because I know something awful has happened. Ivy would never leave him. Never. And as much as I want to give him time to calm, I need to know what went down here.

I rub his back and tip his chin up to face me. "Tell me what happened. Where's mama?"

"She said Mr. Potato Head," Archer sniffs. "That means danger. I had to go hide."

"Ye did a grand job of it," I assure him. "Now can you tell me where your mama was when she said it?"

"We were outside," he croaks. "And the man came to pick us up. We were going to get in the car, but then mama said Mr. Potato Head."

Acid eats at my throat as I consider the possibilities. But there is really only one. The Locos have found her, and I won't stop looking for her until I've flooded the streets of Boston with their blood.

Twenty-Nine

Ivy

"**Y**ou have to know this is a death sentence."

Slick ignores me, going about the business of tying me to a lawn chair. Judging by the amount of time he spent driving around and the lack of foresight on his part, I can tell he's not prepared. The rope he's using is something he dragged out of a janitor's closet, and it's way too stiff to tie a decent knot. He didn't think this through, and I'm eager to convince him of that because it's the only hope I've got.

"You'll bring down the heat of the entire Irish mafia if you do this."

"Not likely," he scoffs. "I don't care who you are, they aren't coming into this territory unless they want war with the locals."

When I swallow, it feels like there's glass stuck in my throat. All this time, I was afraid of the Locos. I thought for sure if someone got me, it would be one of them. But instead it's some random guy who saw me in a club for five minutes and got bent out of shape.

I

My thoughts drift to Archer, and it fractures me to acknowledge that this might be it. After tonight, he won't have a mother. Conor will take care of him, I believe that. It's the only thing I can take comfort in. He cares about him and he will do right by him. But it won't be the same. Archer needs his mom. He needs the softness only a mother can provide in this world.

"I know they did you wrong," I forge on. "They humiliated you. They treated you like crap. And I'm sorry for the way things went down, but it doesn't have to be this way. I can get you money. I can get you whatever you want."

"I don't want your money." Slick scowls. "This isn't a negotiation."

I take a deep breath and plan my words carefully. There's only one thing left to say. One thing that could possibly convince him, even if it's the lie that hurts me the most.

"I'm not just Conor's girlfriend, you know. I'm his wife."

Slick stops fiddling with the rope and looks up at me. "Bullshit."

"It's true," I say. "And if you do this, you will have your revenge for two seconds, but the wrath you will face after ensures you won't live to see next week. You know it's true."

His eyes drift to my hand and he shakes his head. "You're a lying bitch. You don't even have a ring."

"We custom ordered them. I don't have it yet, but that doesn't mean we are any less married. You can look it up if you don't believe me. Check the court records."

Slick hesitates for a split second, and I think I'm getting through to him until he snorts. "He has no idea where you are, and he never will."

The worst part is that it's probably true. I have no idea what Archer will say to Conor when he gets home, but he will be so scared it will be difficult for him to say anything at all. Conor will assume it was the Locos, and by the time he does come looking for me, I'll be long gone.

When Slick finally manages to get the rope wrapped around my wrists, I wiggle against it and he snarls. "Stop fucking moving."

He disappears down a hallway to make a phone call, speaking in a hushed tone that lets me know he's not too far away. We're in a part of the city that looks eerily run down from what I was able to see outside the windows. Slick made me lay back in my seat and told me to shut my eyes the entire ride here, but there's something oddly familiar about this building. The smell, or the peeling paint, or the dread. I can't be sure why I feel that way because I know I've never been here.

We're in a rented office space. Except there is no office. It's just an empty room with a desk, a couple of lawn chairs, and a twin-sized mattress in the corner. On top of the mattress, a pile of tiny bags waits to be distributed. Cocaine, from the looks of it. And that isn't the only place I see it either. On the desk, there are residue lines left behind from what I would guess is Slick.

He mentioned the locals which must mean we are in some kind of gang territory. That doesn't bode well for me, especially if he's running drugs for them. Chances of anyone helping me here are slim to none even if I do manage to escape.

Still, my eyes bounce around the room in search of potential weapons while I try to loosen the rope, but there's next to nothing that I can see. I'm in the middle of trying to edge my chair closer to the desk when Slick returns and shakes his finger at me.

"You aren't very smart, you know that?" He leans down and breathes into my face. "But you do have some spirit, and I've always liked a spirited woman."

I choke back the sickness I feel even looking at him, and he strokes my cheek with a level of creepiness I can't handle. "On second thought, I think I will go back and get your son. If what you say is true, then it's probably best I don't leave any witnesses."

I start to thrash, shaking my head violently as I plead with him.

"He didn't see anything! He won't talk!"

"I'm not a monster." Slick pulls away and checks his watch. "If you do everything I say, I'll make sure the kid goes easy."

"Fuck you!" I scream. "You fucking piece of shit, motherfucker! I will murder you myself—"

His hand cracks across my face, and it feels like my cheek has exploded. The rest of my words die off as his fingers move to my throat, squeezing in warning. "Be quiet you little bitch, or I'll shut you up permanently."

I couldn't talk if I wanted to, and by the time he releases me, I'm left gasping for breath. He isn't about to take any chances, apparently, because he retrieves a piece of cloth from one of the desk drawers and stuffs it into my mouth.

There's a knock from down the hall, and Slick disappears while I try to figure out what to do. It's still early. Conor hasn't been coming home until late. I have little faith that he's home now, which means Archer is alone. And even if Conor's house is secure, it doesn't mean Slick won't find a way in.

Tears stream down my face as I batter my body against the chair, desperate to free myself. But before I make any real progress, Slick returns with another man in tow. The guy is younger, and he shares the same features as the older version. Father and son.

The newcomer lets out a low whistle, and Slick smacks him on the back of the head. "Don't get any bright ideas. She's mine."

Slick's son rolls his eyes. "Whatever."

"Sit down and watch her," Slick commands. "Don't move. Don't call up your buddies or watch TV on your phone. If she makes any noise, choke her until she shuts up. It's real fucking simple, okay? Now can you do that?"

"Sure," the younger man grumbles. "I'm not a fucking idiot."

"I'll be back in an hour tops," Slick says. "Don't fucking touch her. I don't want your sloppy seconds."

He disappears down the hall, and the younger guy smacks his lips together before offering me a lewd smile. "The old man is a pain in my ass sometimes, but he sure knows how to pick em.'"

I spit out the handkerchief and force myself to stay calm. This guy is dumb, just like Slick said. Maybe I can work him. It might be the only chance I have to get out of here.

"I'm Ivy," I tell him. "Who are you?"

"Tut, tut." He shakes a finger at me. "You aren't supposed to be talking, are you?"

I shrug and force a smile. "I just figured you wouldn't mind."

"Well, maybe I do, maybe I don't. And the name is Ronnie, if you really want to know."

His eyes rake over my body, and he makes a show of adjusting the erection in his jeans. He's already thinking about what he wants to do to me, and the thought makes me sick, but that's my opportunity, and I exploit it.

"It seems like your dad doesn't have a lot of respect for you," I observe.

His eyes narrow, and I can tell I've hit a nerve. "Don't talk about what you don't understand. Fucking women, thinking they're all psychologists or some shit."

He paces around the room, lights up a cigarette, and glances at me with every pass he makes.

"I didn't mean to offend you," I say. "I was just thinking, if I had to choose between either of you, I'd much rather have you."

"Oh yeah?" Ronnie smirks. "And why's that?"

I shrug. "You're good looking. You seem like a nice guy. So far you haven't smacked me around or choked me."

His eyebrows pinch together. "Yeah, you're not in for a treat if you don't like the rough stuff. That's all the old man likes."

I cringe, and I can't hide it. Ronnie looks sympathetic to my plight, for all of two seconds. "I wouldn't mind having a taste of you."

I

He blows out a puff of smoke and then extinguishes his cigarette on the desk.

"What's stopping you?" I ask him in a soft voice. "He doesn't have to know."

Ronnie shakes his head. "Can't. The old man would kill me."

But I can tell he's still thinking about it. And when he pulls out his phone and checks the time, I think he might really take me up on it. At least if he unties me, I'll have a shot at fighting him off. I might lose, but I have to try.

That's my plan until Ronnie blows it up by heading for the door. "I have to make a phone call. I'll be right down the hall, so don't even think about moving."

He disappears and doesn't go far, judging from the sound of the porn I can hear playing on his phone while he jerks himself off. It's disgusting, but I've never been more thankful for such a pig. Hopefully he's not a two-pump chump.

I work my chair closer to the desk and snag the rope against the edge in hopes of loosening or fraying it, but it's not working, at least not fast enough. The anxiety is building in my chest, and I'm on the verge of panic as Ronnie's one-man sex show rises to a crescendo.

But something else catches my attention, and it gives me an idea. Ronnie left his cigarettes and lighter on the desk. It's risky, but it's the only hope I've got.

I bend over and contort my body to grab the lighter, but it's not as easy as I'd hoped. It takes me three attempts and precious time. When I finally do get a hold of it, it won't fucking light. There's only a small amount of fluid left inside, and Ronnie's muffled sounds warn me that I'm running out of time.

I shake it, and it finally ignites before I force it between my wrists. I'm expecting a slow, agonizing process, but it takes off so fast I don't have a chance to pull away before the flaming rope singes my shirt.

I jerk my arms apart to avoid burning them, which only manages to cut into my skin. My wrists are raw from the harsh fibers of the rope, but I keep at it, tugging until it finally gives way. When I reach down to untie the knot around my legs, I'm shaking like a leaf. I think I'm in shock, or maybe too much adrenaline. I can't hear Ronnie anymore. He's going to be back any second, and I have nothing to fight him off with.

As I'm pulling out the desk drawer, he comes back, and his face goes white. "What the fuck?"

He comes at me, and I have no choice. I swing it as hard as I can and crack him in the head. Without waiting to assess the damage, I take off running. I can't look back to see if he's behind me.

I can only go forward.

Thirty

Conor

"They aren't talking," Reaper says.

"Then we keep at it until they do," I tell him.

He sighs. We're both soaked in blood, and the two Locos we've got strapped inside his torture room aren't going to last much longer. Logically, I know that. We've already cut off their ears, noses, fingers toes, and any other appendages I didn't think they'd need anymore. All they can tell us is to go fuck ourselves, and I've never felt so desperate.

Ronan sets down his tools and shakes his head. "If they knew where she was, they would have said so by now. I've seen stronger men crack over less."

I pace the floor and throw a glass at the wall, but it doesn't make me feel any better. "Fucks sake, it shouldn't be this hard. We can't stop until we get something. If they touch her—"

"Where's the wee one?" Ronan asks.

"He's upstairs with Rory."

"I think ye need to have another word with him. Ask him what else he can remember."

I don't want to push Archer any more. He's been traumatized enough as it is, but Ronan has a point. If I don't, then the lad might not have a mom by the end of the night.

"I'll keep working on these fellas," Ronan assures me. "You just sort it out with the boy."

I huff it upstairs to Crow's office, zipping up my coat along the way so Archer doesn't see the blood. Rory's got him at Crow's desk, coloring in a book when I walk in.

"Anything?" Rory asks.

I shake my head. "I need to have a quick word with my wee pal."

He nods and sits down on the sofa while I walk around the desk and kneel beside Archer. He looks at me with eyes too innocent to know such pain. "Have you talked to mama yet?"

I can't bring myself to lie to the kid, but it kills me to let him down. "I'm still trying, but I need your help, Archer. Can you do something for me?"

"Yes," he answers. "What should I do?"

"I need you to close your eyes for a second, okay?"

He gives me a funny look, but then does as I asked. "Okay."

"Now I need ye to think about this afternoon. When you and mama were standing on the steps getting ready to leave, do you remember where she said ye were off to?"

"An adventure," he whispers.

"Okay." I rub his back. "That's very good, Archer. Now were you standing outside waiting for a ride?"

"Mama called a cab," he supplies.

"Alright. And did the cab show up?"

"Yes. She was putting our stuff in, but when the guy got out, she told me to go inside."

Something about this just doesn't seem right. I don't see the Locos driving around in a cab trying to nail her. "Do you remember

I

anything about the guy?" I ask. "Can ye tell me what he looked like?"

"He was wearing a cap," Archer says. "And a jacket. I think he hurt his arm."

"Why do you say that?"

"Because it was in one of those things the doctor gives people who hurt their arms."

"Christ," I mutter.

Archer's eyes widen, and I apologize. "Ye did a grand job, little fella. I'm going to go find mama now, okay?"

"Please tell her I miss her," he says.

My throat feels like a vice when I offer him a smile. "I will."

Rory looks at me in question. "What is it?"

"Slick."

Thirty-One

Ivy

Ronnie's footsteps thud down the stairwell behind me, bouncing off the walls as he struggles to regain his balance. He's disoriented, but not disabled.

"I'll shoot you," he yells.

He's gasping for breath in a way that makes me think I seriously hurt him. Either that or he's never exercised in his life. I don't think he has a gun, but even if he did, I can't chance stopping now. Having no idea what I'll find at the bottom of this stairwell, I forge on.

I finally reach the last step and thank every god that might exist because it's a fire exit. And by some miracle, when I press the bar, the door opens. Ronnie curses and I dart out into the night, running as fast as my legs can carry me. Every muscle in my body burns and my calves are seizing up, but I don't care.

I have to do this for Archer. That's what I keep telling myself. I weave my way down dark alleys and side streets, but Ronnie isn't giving up either. I can still hear him behind me, cursing and grunting as he draws nearer. He's catching up to me when I round the corner and see a group of men hanging out in front of an old warehouse.

"Help!" I scream. "Please help me!"

It's dark, and I can't see their faces under the dim street lights, but right now they are my only salvation.

"What the hell is this?" One of shadowed faces asks.

"Don't worry about it," Ronnie answers from behind me. "She's just bent out of shape after an argument. You know how women get."

My legs nearly give out from under me when I come to a stop, and the man at the front of the group steps forward, cocking his head to the side as he examines me. There's a toothpick dangling from his mouth and a funny look in his eyes, and it takes a minute for recognition to curdle in my gut.

It's Muerto's second in charge, Animal. There is no question that he recognizes me too, it's written all over his face. I start to retreat, smacking right into Ronnie. And now, in the ultimate twist of irony, I'm praying that he actually does have a gun.

"You know this bitch?" Animal looks at Ronnie. "Because she's acting like she don't know you."

"Yeah, she's my girlfriend," Ronnie says. "There's no problem here. I'm Slick's son, remember?"

"I remember." Animal scratches at his chin. "But last I checked, she was property of Muerto, God rest his soul."

Before Ronnie can even attempt to formulate an answer, Animal whips out a pistol and fires. Something warm and wet splatters across my face, and I realize with sickening clarity that it's Ronnie's brains. His skull exploded, and he's on the ground, and I'm freaking the fuck out as I my legs lurch into the opposite direction.

I don't make it very far before I'm tackled to the ground with a level of violence that leaves no question about what happens next.

I'm dead.

Thirty-Two

Conor

"Heya, Runt," Dom rumbles through the phone. "Where are you?"

"I'm just down the block from the cab office."

"Don't bother," he says. "The gobshite just showed up here."

"At my house?"

"That would be the one."

"Unfuckingbelievable." I flip a quick bitch and turn the car around. "I'm on my way."

Ten minutes later, I park on the street and beat it up the stairs. Dom left the door unlocked for me and he wasn't shitting me. Slick is inside, hog tied on my parlor floor.

"He really is a fecking eejit," I say.

Dom snorts. "Can honestly say this is a first. I think he came back for the kid."

I remove my jacket and toss it onto the sofa. Slick looks up at me with a fat lip, and I boot him in the stomach to get the show started. "I guess you didn't get the message last time."

He launches into a coughing fit and curls his knees up in an attempt to protect himself. But he won't find me to be a merciful man twice.

"My son will kill her if I'm not back in the hour," he wheezes.

"Doubtful." I kick him in the teeth this time, and he shrieks as blood pours from his mouth. "Unless he wants to die too."

"Fuck you!" Slick garbles. "Fuck you motherfucking son of a bitch!"

I kneel down and meet his eyes. "You have two options here, fuckface. I'll give ye enough credit to believe ye're aware how this ends. You crossed me, and you'll die for it. Simple as that. But you can make it real easy, or real hard."

Slick looks between us, and he knows he's fucked. "Christ, just take her. It's your fucking funeral, I don't care. Take back your little whore—"

I wrap my fingers around his throat and squeeze until his eyes are about to pop out of his head. "Where is she?"

"Highland," he rattles when I let up. "My office on Highland. There aren't any numbers on the building, but the door is green. You can't miss it."

I look to Dom. "Drop him at the club for me, will ye?"

He nods. "Reaper's outside. You're not going alone."

At this point, I wouldn't care. I know where Ivy is, and if I have to burn this city to the ground to get to her, I will.

My heart is beating so hard it feels like I just snorted six kilos of coke, and even worse is the sound of my own thoughts fucking up my head. "You get anything else out of those Locos?"

Reaper shakes his head. "Nah. Squeezed everything I could out of them. They weren't talking."

I turn down Highland and slow to a crawl as we keep a lookout for a green door.

"Have a look at these blockheads." Reaper gestures up ahead.

"What do ye suppose they're doing?"

"I don't know."

Slick's office is in the heart of gangland, and more importantly, Locos territory. They are out on every corner tonight, but from the looks of it, something is going down up ahead. There are three blokes standing guard at the end of an alley, and they're on high alert when they see our headlights. It's too dark for them to make out our faces, but I recognize theirs.

"Pull around the corner," Ronan says.

I pull around the corner and flip a bitch. It's hard to say what's going down in that alley, but it's too coincidental to be ignored.

"I'm not usually a man to shoot first and ask questions later." Reaper starts digging around in the duffle bag he brought with us. "But in this case, it might have to do."

"Aye, I think ye're right."

"Drive by again, slow like," he instructs.

I turn the corner, and Ronan attaches a silencer onto his Glock. We aren't twenty feet away when the tires slow to a creep and he leans against the open window, obscuring the gun beneath his coat sleeve.

The Locos are ready to do battle when they see our car for the second time, and they're pulling out their own pieces when Ronan fires the first shot. His aim is true, even in the dark in a moving car. The first scumbag crumples to the ground before a shot rings out and shatters the front windshield.

I slam on the brakes, and Reaper fires again, spraying the second man as he retreats. I'm already out of the car and chasing the third as he beats it down the alley to duck for cover.

A scream echoes off the surrounding buildings, and a bullet whizzes past my ear, taking some of the flesh with it. Warm blood leaks down my neck, but I forget all about it when I see what's waiting for us at the end of the alley.

Her hair is a mess, and her face is beat to hell, but there's no doubt the half-naked woman is my wife. One of these slimy motherfuckers has his hands wrapped around her throat, and she's trying like hell to fight him off. Her jeans are pulled down, and her shirt is ripped in half, and he's got his dick out still trying to get inside of her.

"Animal!" Someone tries to warn him from behind the dumpster, but it's too late. I'm already there, muzzle pressed against his skull. It's not enough to kill him quickly, but in the grand scheme of things, all that matters is Ivy.

"Get. The. Fuck. Off."

His hands fall away from her throat, and he chuckles as he rocks back onto his knees. "Cool, cool. You must be one of those Irish fuckers, huh? You want to take me out? Why don't you do it like a fucking man. I always hear your crew claiming they're the best fighters in all of Boston. Show me how you do it with your bare hands."

In answer, I aim between his legs and fire a shot, blowing his dick clean off. All his bravado is gone when he collapses into the fetal position and starts simpering like the pussy he is.

"Take it like a fucking man," I taunt him.

My eyes move to Ivy, and I wish they hadn't. The horror in her eyes, the fear… it's too much for me to handle. She's seen me at my worst now, and she can't handle it. She can't handle any of it, which is evident when she rolls onto her side and pukes.

"Fucking Christ." As much as I'd like to toy with Animal and torture him, I need it to be over. For her. I dig into Animal's skull and fire the kill shot. Ivy screams, and I drop to my knees before her.

"They're all spoken for," Reaper interrupts. "But we need to get out of here. You can sort her out in the car."

I scoop Ivy's battered body into my arms and she clings to me, weeping with a brokenness that splinters my ribs and blackens my beating heart.

"It's okay, baby," I whisper. "I'm here now. It's okay."

We pile into the backseat and Ronan burns rubber down the street while I do my best to console Ivy. I right her clothes and pet her hair and kiss her forehead, murmuring my regret for only her.

"I'm so sorry, my love. I'm so fucking sorry. I didn't protect you."

"Archer," she chokes out.

"He's okay. He's safe."

She shakes her head, insistent that he isn't. She won't be okay until she sees him for herself, so I drag my phone out of my pocket and video call Rory. He answers on the second ring.

"Where's the wee one?" I ask.

"He's asleep on the sofa," Rory answers.

"Can you show me?"

He aims the screen at Archer, sound asleep with a blanket and teddy bear, and Ivy releases a breath before she clutches a trembling hand to her mouth to keep from sobbing. It's all she can do. Nothing else matters now because she's my strong girl, and she would take on the whole fucking world if it meant saving her kid.

"Bring him to mine in two hours, would ye?"

Rory agrees, and we disconnect the call. Ivy looks to me, her face dirty, bruised, and swollen.

"Did he touch you?" I rasp. "Did any of them touch you?"

She starts sobbing again, and I think I'm going to be sick, until she shakes her head. She can't get the words out in full sentences, so she gasps them between breaths. "He... almost. Then... you."

"It's okay, baby." I pet her hair and kiss her forehead once more. "It's okay. I won't ever let anyone hurt you again. You have my word that come what may, I will keep you and Archer safe."

She nods against my chest, and I know we still have a lot to talk about, but the first order of business is getting her back to where she belongs.

In our home. With our boy.

Thirty-Three

Ivy

"When is Archer coming?" I croak. My throat is raw from screaming, and I barely have a voice left, but I won't be able to rest until I know he's here and he's safe.

Conor dabs at my face with a wet cloth, cataloging every scratch and bruise with an agony I've never seen in him before. "Rory will bring him shortly. But I think you would agree that we need to get ye cleaned up first. He shouldn't be seeing his mother in such a way."

My eyes water, but I agree. I wouldn't want Archer to see me this way. Conor goes about the task of cleaning my body with a gentleness he doesn't often show. These same hands took life tonight. They shed the blood of Animal and the other Locos, and probably many others before. But when I look up into his soft green eyes, I realize that I don't even fucking care. I don't care about any of it. Not when I know Conor to be good and kind and pure in his own way. This is the man I fell in love with. The one who tends to my wounds and makes everything okay. My love for him is savage and completely irresponsible, but it can't be tamed.

I almost left him, and I almost paid for it with my life.

There is too much space between us, and not even a single inch will do. I want to crawl into his lap and force him to say pretty words and make me promises he will keep. I need him to tell me that he will keep us and love us and never let anything come between us again.

"Is this okay?" His fingers edge the torn hemlines of my sweatshirt, slowly dragging it up to remove it.

I tell him it is, and he busies himself with removing the rest of my tattered clothing, throwing them into the trash where I hope he will burn them. As my eyes wander over him, it occurs to me that he's been so busy taking care of me, he's forgotten to take care of himself.

"Your ear is bleeding."

He brings his fingers up to the wound and shrugs. "Just a flesh wound. I'll live."

"Please put something on it. At least stop the bleeding."

Conor reluctantly agrees, ripping into a fresh pack of gauze and securing it over his ear. It's not the best job, but for now it will have to do. I want to help him, but I'm too sore to move on my own and the pain is catching up with me now. I realize it when he walks to the bath and tests the water and I'm left to support myself on the edge of the sink.

"Feels good," he says. "Let's get you inside."

"I can't," I whimper.

Conor turns to me, and when he recognizes the pain in my eyes, he comes back to me without delay. "It's okay, love. I've got you."

I fall against his chest, too weak to wrap my arms around him. But it doesn't matter. His skin against mine is all that I need. I need him to stay with me like this all night, and I hope that he will.

Conor unbuttons his jeans and kicks them off, and then holds me upright with one arm while he strips off his shirt. He doesn't bother to remove his briefs before gathering me up into his arms and carrying me to the tub.

"That's it, love." He lowers us both into the tub and settles us into the warm water. "Just relax. I've got you."

I melt into him, and even though I'm still a fucking mess, a deranged smile curves my lips. I can only imagine what we must look like. This big, burly man crammed into the tiny bathtub with me. It can't be comfortable for him, but he doesn't complain. He doesn't seem to give it any thought at all as he soaps a cloth and scrubs it over my skin, pausing to ask if the pressure is okay. He asks me where I hurt, and then he feels those places with his fingers. When it's all said and done, his level of care says everything words can't. He touches me like I'm his salvation. Like he couldn't live without me, and it took us almost losing each other for him to understand that.

He massages me, strong fingers kneading the tension from my back and shoulders. Then his lips are on my neck, kissing me, breathing me in. We're melded together, and all the wrong from the night is somewhere else, in another time and place where we don't exist. And when he finally does choke out some words, it's all I ever need to know.

"I'm so sorry, baby. I'm so fucking sorry. I love you, Ivy. You can't ever leave me like that again."

Thirty-Four

Conor

"**M**ommy!" Archer cries out.

My beautiful girl can barely move, but she musters every last ounce of strength left in her to wrap her arms around her son. "I'm here," she tells him. "I'm here, my love."

They hold each other for as long as Ivy can handle, but when it becomes too much for her, I intervene. "It's been a long day. Why don't we all go to bed."

Ivy nods, and I help them both settle into our bed. But when I stand up, her arm shoots out to catch me. "Please don't leave."

"I'm not going anywhere, love," I assure her. "I'm just taking off my shirt."

Her eyes never leave me until I'm tucked in behind her, an arm wrapped around her waist while Archer curls against her chest. In this space between darkness and dawn, I have a clarity I've never felt before. A purpose in life that is so much more than my brotherhood, or proving myself, or anything else that ever seemed important before.

My whole life is in this room. This is my family, and I'll never let myself forget how close I came to losing them because of my own ignorance and pride.

I bury my face against Ivy, breathing her in as I kiss her hair. "I love you, baby girl. I love you both."

<hr/>

"Conor?" Ivy's panicked voice escalates from inside the bedroom, and I fling open the shower door, barely managing to cover myself with a towel before I make it back to her.

"What's wrong, love?"

She looks up at me and blinks, disoriented and confused, but worst of all... terrified. The covers are clutched around her, and she is too paralyzed to move, but it's clear she thought I left her.

I walk over to her, still dripping wet, and kneel down before her. "It's okay now, love."

My fingers feather over the only patch of skin left unscathed on her battered face. It looks worse in the daylight, and the only comfort I have is the knowledge that I will drain the life from Slick's eyes. But if I could, I would murder Animal all over again, and I would make him suffer in ways he's never known.

"I thought you left," Ivy blurts. "I woke up and you weren't here."

"I'm not going anywhere," I promise her. "I was just taking a shower."

She still looks unsettled, and I'm sure we have many more days like this ahead of us.

"Ronan and Dom are just down the hall too. Nobody is getting in here, love."

She glances at the door to the hall. "They are?"

"Aye. But if you don't feel safe here, then we'll move. We'll buy a new house."

She bites her lip, and nothing comes out, but in her heart, I know that's what she needs to move forward. Ivy still has to wrap her head around the notion that it's my job to look after her. She wouldn't ever come right out and tell me she wanted a new house because that costs money. But I want her to know these boundaries between us aren't going to remain. Whatever it takes to make her feel secure in my love and devotion for her, I will do it.

I lean up and give her a gentle kiss. "Besides, we'll need a bigger place when I get you in a family way."

A blush spreads over her cheeks, and I kiss her for real this time. She tastes so fucking sweet I never want to stop, but I don't want to hurt her either.

"How do ye feel about a shower?"

"I'm a little sore," she says. "But I think I can manage it."

She glances back at Archer, still asleep, and worry passes over her face.

"He'll be okay," I tell her. "If you want, I can have Ronan come sit with him."

She thinks on it for a minute. "Maybe. I just don't want him waking up alone."

I pop my head out into the hall and call for Ronan, and he appears a moment later. With my instructions, he sits on the end of the bed and folds his hands in his lap with the seriousness of a sentry. Ivy takes one look at him and knows that nobody will ever fuck with our boy if they have to contend with Ronan.

I help her from the bed and we make a slow walk back into the bathroom. All she has on from last night is one of my tee shirts, and it fits like a dress on her. I help her out of it, trying not to look at her body because right now would be an inopportune time to get an erection. But regardless of my precautions, my dick throbs between my legs, itching to get back inside of her.

I test the water with my hands to make sure it's still warm and then help Ivy inside. She relaxes into me completely and the ugliness

I

of this past week disappears with the knowledge that she trusts me. Even after she saw me at my worst, she trusts me.

"Ivy, there's something I need to ask you."

"What is it?" She twists her neck to look up at me.

"We have Slick, but I've yet to deal with him. There isn't a question that he'll die, but I need to know what he did. I need to know how he should suffer."

Her fingers curl into my back and she buries her head in my chest. "He didn't get far enough to do anything."

Satisfied with that answer, I rub small circles into her back, and her lip trembles. "But he was going to take my son. *My son.* He was going to—" She chokes back a sob, and I hold her until she's calm enough to speak again. "I just want him dead. I want him gone. Does that make me a monster?"

My fingers brush over her cheek and down her throat. "No, love, it doesn't. You won't ever have to think of him again. I'll make him go away."

Tears splash against her cheeks, and I try to brush them away, but she shakes her head. "I'm sorry I left, Conor. It was so stupid."

"I fucked up, love. That's on me. I'm not used to being so out of sorts over someone. I think we just need to get better at fighting."

"What you said last night," she whispers. "Did you mean it?"

My lips graze against hers, longing to taste her. "I meant it then, and I mean it now. Ye're mine, baby girl, and I love you."

She squeezes me and offers me a watery smile. "I love you too."

My heart beats victorious in my chest, and I groan into her mouth when she reaches up and pulls my face back to hers.

"I need you, Conor," she pleads. "I want you inside of me. I have to feel you."

"Christ." I pull away and look at her. "Are you sure? You just—"

"I don't care. I miss you and I need you. I just need to feel good. Please."

My dick is so hard I could drill a hole through the shower wall, but I'm still nervous. "We can try, but if it hurts at all, we're stopping."

"Okay," she concedes.

I want inside of her now. It's been so long, and I just want to plunge my cock into her warmth again and again. When I slide my fingers between her legs, she's already wet for me.

Ivy moans and arches into me, and I know she won't be able to sustain an orgasm when it's all she can do to keep herself upright. So, I gather her up into my arms and wrap her legs around my hips, holding onto her arse to keep her in place.

Her arms fall around my shoulders, giving me open access to her beautiful tits, so perfect I want to worship them all morning. I start by licking her nipples, sucking them into my mouth and drinking in her sweetness as she squirms in my arms.

"So fucking beautiful," I groan.

My impatient little vixen reaches down and wraps her palm around my cock, and my vision darkens at the sight of it. Her petite fingers don't even close around the girth, and yet she takes me inside of her like a fucking champion.

"You keep doing that, and I won't make it inside of you," I tease.

She smiles at me warmly. "Then quit torturing me and give me what I need."

With a request like that, how could I not? I pry my cock from her hand and rub it obscenely against her wet pussy. My balls are so tight they feel spring loaded, and I'm doubtful how long I'll survive once I get inside her.

"Conor," she whines.

I squeeze the head of my dick into her tight hole, and she shudders, wiggling her hips until she sinks down and bottoms out.

"Christ," I rumble, reaching down to grope her. "Ye're so tight baby. I need you to come for me before I blow my fucking load."

Her nails dig into my back and she bites down on my shoulder in an attempt to stay quiet while I finger her clit. Ivy needs this as much as I do, and it doesn't take her long. The orgasm rips through her with a violence that leaves her panting for breath, and I'm already fucking her before the aftershocks end.

So wet, and warm, and mine. I thrust up into her again and again, squeezing her ass as my eyes fall shut and my head lolls back. I can't speak. I can't do anything but ride out of the wave as hot come spurts from my dick into her womb, filling her. Claiming her.

We are both breathless and spent when I come back down from the high, mauling her lips with a possession I refuse to water down.

"Mine," I utter. "Only mine."

Thirty-Five

Conor

"How is he?"

Alexei arches a brow at me. "I'd venture a guess that he's pretty sore."

A smile curves across both our faces as Boris walks out of the room, a cigarette hanging between his lips as he zips up his trousers. "I think I've taken my fill of pleasure. He's boring me now."

"They always bore you when they stop screaming," Alexei muses.

They laugh, and I nod to Boris. "Thank you for your service."

"Anytime," he puffs out between drags.

The Russians are our allies, and Boris has helped us out many a time when the situation warranted it. Our brotherhood is a firm believer in an eye for an eye, and even though Slick might not have touched Ivy, he certainly intended to. There is only one suitable punishment for such a crime. When I open the door and find his limp body draped over a wooden bench, I have no remorse for his agony.

"You," he slurs, eyes opening half mast. "Fucking kill me or let me go you sadistic fuck."

"As you wish." I pull out my Glock and tap it against my thigh. "Just one question though. What exactly were your intentions with the boy?"

Slick makes an unintelligible sound, and I can see the wheels turning in his pea sized brain. He knows what's coming, and I don't expect honesty from him, but it can't hurt to ask.

"I wouldn't have harmed him. It was just a matter of keeping her compliant."

"Aye." I curl my lip in disgust. "You would. What honor do ye have left? Ye're going to die, there's nothing left to lose now."

"I don't hurt kids," Slick insists.

"To be sure, ye don't hurt my kid."

His lips flatten, and he's practically frothing at the mouth to challenge me on that, but he knows better.

"Blood or not, that boy is my son," I inform him. "And you should know what happens when ye touch a brother's son."

"I didn't touch him." Slick thrashes against his restraints with what little life he has left.

"But ye thought about it. That was enough."

I stuff the Glock back into my jeans and reach for my knife instead. Slick breathes harder in anticipation, flinching when I step nearer. He's wrong if he thinks it's going to be a violent attack. Slow and steady wins the race.

I cut the rope from his waist and use it to secure the knots between his wrists and ankles. A quick call out to Boris, and he opens the door and lets Alexei inside with the wheelbarrow.

"What the fuck now?" Slick yelps. "Just finish me already."

"I intend to."

Not so gingerly, I dump the sack of shite face down into the wheelbarrow. He doesn't say a word, but he's shaking as we wheel him down the dark tunnel in Alexei's basement. When we reach the exit, the sun is high and it's a beautiful day for a funeral.

Slick wastes his energy carrying on the entire way to the fresh slice of earth in the woods where many a traitor has come to meet his maker. The freshly excavated hole is six feet deep, and Alexei seems to appreciate my efforts.

"You didn't skimp on the details," he says. "This is good."

Without further ado, we each grab one side of the barrow and unceremoniously dump Slick into the hole.

"Come on, man," he screeches. "You can't do me like this. Have a heart."

The two of us grab our shovels and start the long process of covering his body with dirt. He bitches and moans about it the entire time, and I don't bother to acknowledge any of it until we're ready to cover his face.

"For every minute you still have breath in your lungs, I want you to think about my wife and my son. Think about how sorry you are that you even considered laying a hand on them."

"I'm sorry," he blurts. "So fucking sorry."

His wasted words are smothered by a shovel full of dirt on his face. After that, Alexei and I work in silence, burying Slick and sending a message to anyone else who thinks they can take what's mine.

Thirty-Six

Ivy

"What do you think?"

Archer glances around the room and shrugs. "It's nice, mama."

I can't help but laugh when I meet Conor's eyes. The house is a lot more than nice. It's more than I ever could have dreamed of having. Conor told me to pick out a house, any house I wanted, and even if I never said it out loud, he knew this was the one. The Victorian style townhouse is in the Beacon Hill neighborhood, only a few doors down from some of his other friends. I feel safe here, as Conor intended, and I hope Archer does too.

After moving all day, we're exhausted and ready to settle into our new space. But Conor and I still have plans to celebrate. I get Archer tucked into bed and go over my instructions with Rory again. I don't think I'll ever stop being nervous about letting him out of my sight, but over the past two months, I've come to understand that Conor was right. These guys protect their own and they won't let anything happen to Archer, or even me, on their watch.

"You ready, hot mama?" Conor wraps his arms around me from behind and feathers his lips over the length of my neck.

"I think so." I turn into him and drag his mouth to mine, kissing him like it's our last day on earth. Conor grunts and pulls away with a wicked smile.

"If ye keep at that, we won't be making it out the door."

He threads his fingers through mine and leads me to the car. He gave me warning this time, so I already know where we're going. And for Conor, I'm ready to try again. This is important to him, so I try not to let my nerves get the best of me as he drives us to Sláinte.

The drive is far too short, and when we pull into the parking lot, Conor turns off the ignition, but doesn't get out of the car. Now he's the one who looks nervous, and it's totally freaking me out.

"I have something for you," he says. "A couple things actually."

"Oh." I rasp. "What is it?"

An awkward laugh rumbles from his chest as he taps his fingers against the steering wheel. "Chrissakes, this is ridiculous. I'm fumbling like a schoolboy."

"It's okay," I insist. "Whatever it is, you can tell me."

Warmth bleeds into his eyes, and it must be infectious because I feel it in my chest too.

"I just want ye to know this wasn't the way I intended for it to go down. I wanted to give it to ye earlier, but with the moving and everything, there was never a perfect time. You deserve something more romantic, but I'm not very good at that stuff."

He reaches into his pocket and pulls out a small black box, and my heart beats wildly in anticipation. Conor doesn't think he's romantic, but he has no idea how much that isn't true. Because when he looks at me with that boyish smile and flips open the box, I couldn't imagine anything better than this.

"Sorry it's taken me so long to sort ye out a proper ring, but I wanted it to be just right."

I examine the vintage diamond ring through bleary eyes, nodding my approval. "It's beautiful."

"It's an antique, but if you don't like it, we can get ye a different one. I just liked the story that came with this."

"What story?" I ask.

"This ring belonged to a couple who were mad about each other. They came from two different worlds and didn't have a lick in common. She was a society girl, and he was the son of a farmer with barely two nickels to rub together. Against her family's protests, they ran off and got married, and then he was sent off to war."

"What happened to them?" I press. "Did he live?"

"He was captured and presumed dead," Conor says. "For six years, they told her that was so, but she couldn't believe it. She never took off the ring. She never gave up hope. And then one day out of the blue, he appeared on their doorstep. They spent the next fifty years together and died within days of each other. She wore the ring for all that time, vowing that as long as she kept it on, he would always come back to her."

"Wow." I can't tell if I'm more moved by the story or the emotion on Conor's face. "That's really sweet."

"We Irish tend to believe in good luck charms, and this will be ours." He slides the ring onto my finger, and I examine the stone, noting that it's new. But the original art deco style of the band is untouched.

"I made a few minor changes," Conor explains. "I hope ye like it."

"Like it?" I take his hand in mine and squeeze. "I love it. It's the most beautiful thing anyone has ever given me. I don't even know what to say."

He offers me a lazy smile. "It was long overdue. I want the world to know ye're mine, and I'm yours."

"Oh, God, I need to get you a ring."

He pulls another box from his pocket and wiggles it between his fingers. "Already got that covered, love. Would ye care to do the honors?"

I open the box and inspect the ring he bought. A simple black titanium band. I couldn't have picked something better for him myself. I slide it onto his ring finger with some difficulty, considering his huge knuckles, and we both laugh.

"Thank you, Conor. This means so much to me."

His fingers brush the length of my arm, making me shiver. "Thank you for being my wife. I like to fancy myself the luckiest man on this planet."

My lips graze against his. "I think we're both the lucky ones."

He kisses me, and it's the kind of kiss that turns my insides all gooey. It's deep and possessive and intense, a complete symphony of all that Conor is. I don't think I'll ever tire of kissing this man. Making out in parked cars or sneaking into dark corners to frantically tear at each other's clothes. He makes me feel like a teenager, love drunk in the best possible way.

"Shite," Conor grunts. "Ye got me all worked up."

He adjusts the erection in his jeans, and I smirk as my fingers drag over his zipper. "You know, there's a solution for that."

His eyes darken, and five minutes later, he's fucking my mouth like the caveman he is. He fingers me beneath the curtain of my dress, and we both come violently. I'm still riding the high when I collapse back against his seat to catch my breath. I finger comb my hair in the mirror and wipe away the mascara that leaked from my eyes while Conor watches.

"I guess we should probably go inside, huh?"

Conor is quiet, seemingly lost in his own thoughts.

"Everything okay?" I ask.

"Aye." He nods. "There was just something else I was thinking about. It might seem silly to you, but it would mean a lot to me."

I

"What is it?"

He reaches out and toys with the ring on my hand. "You took my last name, and I want that for Archer too. I want him to know that even if I'm not his real father, I'm always going to be his dad."

My heart squeezes as a million different emotions detonate inside of it. Before I can even make sense of what's happening, I'm wiping away my own mess of tears. "You want to adopt him?"

"Aye," Conor answers. "We're a family. We should all have the same name. I don't want him growing up with a blank space on his birth certificate or thinking that he's not my son, because he is in every way but that one."

"That's incredible..." I say. "I can't think of anything he'd like better than to call you his dad."

Conor recognizes the worry in my eyes, and he doesn't gloss over it. "But?"

I stare down at our hands, unified, and everything about it feels so right. There's no longer a question in my mind about my relationship with Conor or if he loves Archer. But I'm still a mother, and I'm always going to worry.

"I guess I'm just nervous," I admit. "I'm honored to call you my husband and a father to Archer. You are who you are, and I love you for that. But I want Archer to have a normal life. I don't want him growing up to—"

"Become a gangster," Conor finishes for me.

"Yes." I shrug.

"I want the best for him too, Ivy," he says. "The kid's smart. He can do anything he wants. Go to school, become an accountant or a doctor. Whatever. It's up to him. I'm not going to force his hand on anything."

I meet his eyes and only see truth there. It's the reassurance I needed. I already know Conor will protect us. He will keep us safe, and he will give Archer a good life. Maybe it's crazy for me to accept that I'm married to the mob, but I don't care. This is what I want. It's what Archer wants. And for the first time in my life, I'm doing what really feels best for us.

"You'll need to ask him," I say. "It's up to him."

Conor gives me a goofy smile. "Aye, I can do that."

I lean over and kiss him again, and he nips his way down my neck, breathing in my ear. "I think the lads are ready to meet my wife. What do ye say?"

I close my eyes and breathe him in. "I'd say it's about time."

Epilogue

Conor

"What in the bleeding hell is wrong with your woman?" Dom asks.

I glance across the room at Ivy, who's perched against the table nibbling on a saltine cracker. "I've got no clue. She's been a little on the cranky side. Last night she started crying over a cartoon."

Crow smirks like he knows something I don't before he leans back and takes a drink from his glass. "Welcome to the club. Ye best get used to it."

Dom laughs and my eyes drift back to my wife. Even though she hasn't exactly been her usual self, I have nothing but warmth for her when I catch her mingling with the other wives like it's second nature. She's in my world now, and I never have to question that she wants to be anywhere else because even when we nitpick or nag about stupid shite, at the end of the day, we always come back to each other.

Every night, before her eyes fall shut and her breathing evens out and I ask myself again how I came to have everything I never knew

I wanted, she tells me that she loves me. And I know she means it. When I have a rough day, I don't have to say anything to her. She just knows. She's there for me when I open the door, and she does everything in her power to make it all okay. For me, and Archer, and anyone else she cares about. The woman might weigh a hundred pounds soaking wet, but she's got a heart of pure gold.

"She can be cranky," I tell the lads. "I don't care. She's still mine."

Dom shakes his head like he's disgusted, but I know he gets it. They all get it. Because we might be Kings on the streets, but we would be nothing without our Queens at home.

"Dad!" Archer squeals as he bounds through the parlor with red cheeks. He's out of breath, and half his mouth is still painted in chocolate from the cake, and I've never been so proud as I am when I hear those three letters from his lips.

"What's up, little fella?" I grunt when he leaps onto my lap.

"Mama said to ask you if I can open presents now!"

"Aye." I tap him on the nose with a smile. "That sounds about right."

He disappears just as soon as he arrived to tackle the mountain of presents that's accumulated in the middle of the parlor. One thing about birthday parties in this family is that there is no such thing as telling the lads they can't spoil your kids. It's going to happen no matter what, so you might as well just accept it.

Ivy comes to stand beside me while Crow takes the lead and distributes each present, announcing who it's from and letting Archer tear into it. Over the next twenty minutes, we watch him unwrap a battery powered BMW, a hand-controlled drone, Wheelies, a Nerf Go Kart, and enough Legos to ensure I'll never walk across the floor without cursing again. Ivy's eyes widen with each gift that's unwrapped, but when it comes to the tiny motorcycle, I can't help laughing at the panic on her face.

"We'll save that one for a little later," I whisper to her. She gives me an exhausted smile before I pull her into my lap and kiss the side of her temple.

The party goes on well into the evening, and by the time the last of our guests leaves, my wife can barely keep her eyes open. Archer already passed out from the excitement of the day when I carry her back to our bedroom and lay her down.

"You okay?" I brush the hair away from her face.

"Yes," she answers. "Are the parties always that intense?"

"Aye." I smirk. "Family is important. It means a lot to the lads to give the kids a smile when they can."

"It's the best birthday he's ever had," she mumbles sleepily. "Thank you."

I lean down and kiss her, and then I try to get up with the intentions of cleaning up the kitchen. I don't want it to fall on Ivy's shoulders when I have to go back to work in the morning and she's not feeling well.

"Conor." She grabs my arm and rolls onto her side, propping herself up with her elbow. "We'll have another birthday to celebrate soon."

I think she might be delirious, but I count off the months in my head to both of our birthdays, which are still a good six months away. "Whose?"

She offers me a nervous smile as she pats her tummy. "This little nugget right here."

For a minute, I can't even breathe. I want to make sure I heard her right, but there are a thousand thoughts crashing through my mind at the same time. "Ye're pregnant?"

She bites her lip. "Is that... good?"

I kneel down beside the bed and cup her face, smashing my lips against hers in answer. I kiss her with the passion of a man who's just won the lottery. I kiss her until neither of us can breathe, and then I leave her panting in a heap on her pillow as I worship her throat with my mouth.

My hand slides across her belly, cupping the small bump there. I'd noticed it, but I just thought she was finally putting on the weight she'd lost. "How long do we have?"

"Six more months." Her fingers thread through my hair as she massages my scalp. "That's good, right?"

"Baby, you have no idea. That's it. I'm done now. You've given me everything I wanted."

She laughs and shakes her head as I climb up onto the bed beside her.

"So, that's why I've been moody. It's hormones."

"You can be as moody as you want," I assure her. "You just focus on growing this wee baby of ours, and I'll take care of everything else."

I mean it, and I can't wait to show Ivy just how much I mean it when she curls into me and rests her head on my beating heart.

"I'm going to take care of you," I murmur. "Always, my love."

Bonus Epilogue

Conor

"What do ye mean her doctor won't be able to make it?" I glare.

The bloke standing at my wife's feet barely acknowledges me because his eyes are laser focused on her treasure chest and I'm about ready to loaf him in the head.

"She's out of town," the doctor says. "I'm on call, and this baby is coming now. So, if you'll excuse me, I need to help your wife."

"Conor," Ivy hisses between labored breaths. "It's fine."

"It's not fine," I insist. "He keeps staring at you."

The doctor looks at me and shakes his head like I'm the one who's mad.

"He has to stare at me," Ivy insists. "There's a baby coming out of me in case you haven't noticed. Now do you want to help me or not?"

When I meet her eyes and recognize the pain she's in, it occurs to me what a blockhead I'm being. But I still don't like it. I don't want this tosser anywhere near her.

"Oooooh," she groans.

I forget what I'm even worked up about as I scramble to her side and take her hand in mine. "It's okay, love. Ye're doing a great job."

She hisses out a few more breaths and squeezes her eyes shut as the pervert masquerading as a doctor issues instructions. I can't hear a word of it because I'm focused on my wife. My beautiful wife who's giving birth to our child.

I smooth her hair back and kiss her forehead hoping to soothe her, but her body seizes up again and she whacks me in the face when her head jolts forward.

"Oh, God, Conor." She blinks, horrified, and I don't understand what's happening until I feel it running down my face.

Warm blood pours from my nose, the metallic taste painting my lips. Right about the same time, I hear the doctor saying something about one last push. And then I glance down between Ivy's legs where it looks like the floor of Reaper's basement.

Blood. *So much blood.*

It's the last thought I have before I hit the floor.

⟳

"Archer, meet your little sister, Keeley."

"Keeley," he repeats, eyes wide with wonder as he squeezes into the space next to me.

I wrap my free arm around the little lad and hold them both while Ivy watches with a sleepy smile across the room.

"Ye're a big brother now," I say to Archer. "That means you must always look out for your sister and protect her. Do ye understand what that means?"

Archer nods as his fingers smooth over her tiny forehead. "I'll look after her like you look after us, Dad. I'll read her bedtime stories and when she's older make sure she eats her vegetables too."

I smile and give him a little squeeze.

"Excuse me." The nurse pops her head in. "But I can't hold them off anymore. Do you mind if they come in now?"

I look to Ivy, and she laughs, nodding along. "They can come in now."

Before the nurse can even extricate herself, the room is full of my brothers and their wives, and they've all come bearing gifts. The boxes and bags get abandoned to the side of the room as they take their turns holding the wee one and posing for photos like they aren't the most fearsome men this side of Boston.

"Looks like ye did a grand job of it." Crow eyes my bandaged nose. "Even if you did come out a with a battle wound."

"I'll do better next time," I assure him.

He smirks and removes a flask from his coat, and we toast to Keeley's health and to our family. And it is a family. Everything I love is right here in this room, and I would do anything to protect it. When I meet Ivy's eyes, I know she understands it too.

"You've given her a life worth fighting for." Crow squeezes my shoulder. "It's about goddamn time."

The End.

Works by
A. ZAVARELLI

Boston Underworld Series
CROW: Boston Underworld #1
REAPER: Boston Underworld #2
GHOST: Boston Underworld #3
SAINT: Boston Underworld #4
THIEF: Boston Underworld #5

Sin City Salvation Series
CONFESS: Sin City Salvation #1

Bleeding Hearts Series
Echo: A Bleeding Hearts Novel Volume One
Stutter: A Bleeding Hearts Novel Volume Two

Twisted Ever After Series
BEAST: Twisted Ever After #1

Standalones
Tap Left
Hate Crush

For a complete list of books and audios,
visit www.azavarelli.com/books

Made in the USA
Columbia, SC
10 May 2023

16348668R00104